Nickel City

N. Sullivan

First Print Edition 2014

ISBN: 0615960189

ISBN-13: 978-0615960180

Published by Sixty Six Underground

www.nsullivan.co

To Mom and Dad and my family, for literally everything.

To Jane, without whom this book would be an utter mess of fragments and misused colons. Best. Editor. Ever.

Thanks to M.C. Shipley, who bravely waded into this print edition and exceeded expectations. You've earned a scone.

Without all of you, this book never would have happened.

Chapter 1

Blood money. Remember it was blood money. Not protecting the innocent, not doing the right thing. Simple. Mercenary. Blood money. A dark alley. Running. Gunshots, thick accented voices coming from behind, getting closer. The smell of stagnant water, a canal lapping against wooden piles. Yellow glints on polished steel in street lamps. Shots, a scream, a ricochet. Pain. Incredible burning pain. Screaming. Endless screaming.

Tommy's eyes opened. The nightmare again. The circular scar on his left hand burned as he forced himself off of the mattress. He looked at the clock; it was five a.m. He usually didn't get up this early, but he knew sleep wouldn't return.

The past few months that damn nightmare had come almost every night. It woke him up every morning more or less at five a.m. He thought about taking a sleeping pill, but it probably wouldn't help.

Walking across the concrete floor, he made his way to the closet of his one room apartment. Opening the door, the blue early morning light coming through the soot-stained wire-reinforced glass windows on the other side of his bedroom cast a dim light on the small altar and two votive candles, partially used. Tommy entered the closet, lit the candles and kneeled down as he shut the door.

Two hours later he had exercised and showered. He walked back into the bedroom and started getting dressed. Looking in the mirror, he combed his thick dark brown hair. It contrasted pretty badly with his pale skin and light blue eyes, but he still had the jaw line of a matinee movie star. The alarm next to his bed went off as he tightened his tie. He looked at his pocket watch. It was old, an antique by now. The gold-plated cover was worn through to the brass. He wondered why he still carried it as he locked the clasp of his wristwatch on his right wrist. It didn't seem to serve much of a purpose anymore. The cold metal felt good in his hand though, familiar. He locked the fob on his vest button and slipped the watch into his pocket.

Now dressed, he made his way down to the first floor office. The sun had come up, and warm light was pouring through the smoked glass door. Tommy unlocked a file cabinet in the back office and pulled out a stuffed manila envelope. Just holding the envelope made his skin crawl a little. More blood money, another mercenary job. Life was a revolving door of this shit, and Tommy didn't know who he hated more for it-himself or the people who paid him. His client wanted these pictures, but as far as Tommy was concerned, there was nothing more disgusting than what was in that envelope. He locked the door behind him and walked to his car.

Downtown, he sat in a posh office looking across a polished antique desk at the man who had hired him. Even now, as the man thumbed through the images in that envelope, Tommy was disgusted. The man smiled.

"My lawyer is going to have a field day with this. There's no way that bitch is going to be able to play innocent in front of the judge when he's staring at these." The man pulled out a checkbook and scribbled out a check. "This should cover your expenses, Mr. White."

Tommy picked the check up off the desk.

"This is too much. I quoted you five thousand. I expected five thousand."

"Well, consider the rest a tip. With the ammunition you've given me, you saved me millions; I think that's worth an extra five grand." The man smiled. Even his smile was greasy.

Tommy put the check in his pocket.

"We're done now. You won't be hearing from me again, unless this check bounces." He stood and walked toward the door. "Good luck in court."

Rain battered the awning over his head. Everything glistened. Tommy watched from across the street as the young woman got out of the cab. He had been standing here half the night, waiting for her to get home. He took a deep breath and crossed toward her.

"Mrs. Evans? Sarah Evans?" He saw her choke back tears.

"It's Smith, or at least will be soon." She stepped under the awning of her temporary apartment and closed her umbrella. Not a terrible place, but nothing like what she was used to.

"Yes, I know you just came from your husband's lawyer's office. I have something for you." He reached into his coat and pulled out a manila envelope.

"What is this?"

"Photographs, from six months ago. They're of your husband. The negatives are in there. Give them to your attorney." Tommy could feel her staring as he walked away. Now at least some of the blood on his hands was righteous. After all, he had already cashed Mr. Evans' check. Tommy walked back to his car and drove back to the office.

* * *

A week later, he was awake before the alarm again. This time, however, there was a sound he didn't recognize coming from the front of the building. Someone knocking on the door? *His* door? That didn't generally happen. Tommy went through the checklist: The bills were paid, no outstanding warrants, Jehovah's Witnesses didn't come to businesses, the bums knew better, he didn't meet new clients here, in fact, since that stunt he pulled with the Evans' divorce, he didn't expect to have any clients anytime soon. So who was knocking on his door at 6:30 in the morning?

Tommy went to the one clean window in the building. He kept it that way just for this. Looking down onto the sidewalk, he saw a young woman, Asian, looking around nervously. That was nothing to note, in this neighborhood he'd be more worried if she wasn't nervous.

Either way, she should get off the street. Tommy got dressed and walked down to the office. She was banging on the glass when he got to the door.

"What is it?"

"Mr. White? Jim White, the private detective?"

"Yes."

She pushed her way past him and set her coat on the torn vinyl of one of the old steel office chairs. "I'm sorry to bother you so early, but I really need your help."

Tommy looked her over. Twenty five, maybe? Office worker by the look of her hands and her fashionable glasses. Athletic, but still slight. Right around five foot three. Up all night.

"Wait. First off, who are you?"

"I'm sorry." She offered her hand. "Katrina Liu."

"Jim White, but you already knew that. Take a seat, Ms. Liu."

"It's Doctor Liu, actually. I'm a physicist at the University of Buffalo."

Tommy had a little trouble believing that. Looking at her, he figured she couldn't be much over twenty four. He offered her a chair. She sat quickly. She seemed to do everything quickly.

"You want some coffee? I was about to make my morning pot." Tommy blew the dust out of his coffee cup and removed a pile of papers from the top of the coffee maker. The ancient machine didn't actually make coffee anymore. He didn't know what was wrong with it. But it did heat water that was just right for instant.

"No, thank you. I'm a little tense right now. I think someone's following me."

"Is that why you're here to see me? That sounds more like a matter for the police."

"They're already involved. But there's more to it."

Tommy sipped from his cup of nasty, bitter coffee, then decided it was better not to. He set it next to the machine, sat on the edge of the small reception desk cluttered with maps and legal documents that had never been filed.

"Do tell."

"A few weeks ago, someone broke into my lab, smashed my equipment, and killed Roger."

"Who's Roger?"

"My lab assistant. He's, well, he *was* twenty-two." Her eyes lowered as she spoke. She felt guilty about his death.

"So what do the police say? Any leads?"

"They have one suspect. Me."

"They think you did it?"

"Yes, they think I smashed my own lab *and* killed Roger."

Tommy wondered for a moment. His relationship with the local cops may not have been the greatest, but in normal cases, they usually got their shit right.

"I didn't do it, Mr. White. The only reason they think it was me is that someone used my key code to get into the lab."

"Wait, wait, wait. Let's go back a few steps. You should be talking to a lawyer, not a detective. And while we're on the subject, how did you find me? I'm not exactly in the phone book."

"I already hired a lawyer. He told me to try to think of other people who could have been involved. That's the best he can do for now." She wrung her hands. "As far as how I found you, well, to be honest, I've known about you for a while now."

"Really. And why would that be?" Tommy moved around behind the desk to the filing cabinet. Trying to be as nonchalant as possible, he opened the top drawer. Flipping through files like he was looking for a document, he double-checked that his guns were where he left them.

"Well, I collect antiques. I prefer to collect the everyday objects, things that have seen use. When you almost outbid me for a severely damaged nineteenth century captain's spyglass at Christie's last year, I did a little research and found that you and I have similar interests." Tommy remembered the spyglass, one of a set. How did she know he had been the other bidder?

"In what, exactly?"

"Dark energy."

"Dark what?"

"Dark energy."

"I'm afraid I don't follow."

"Scientists have believed in its existence for years, but they've been looking for it the wrong way. It's like nothing anyone's ever seen. It's some kind of radiation, but not like any radiation that has been documented. This is *completely new.* It seems to hang in space, not travel in straight lines like normal particles. I found a way to detect large collections of this radiation when they form. It's a sudden spike in background noise I call a burst. I still don't know why or how it bursts, but it seems to do so at random, and without the usual fallout you would expect from high energy particles. There's no destruction, no reports of radiation sickness or burns on people who were nearby, nothing."

Tommy nodded his head, pretending to understand as she continued.

"While I was in the early stages of research, Roger noticed that every radiation spike we logged seemed to be in the area in and around

Buffalo.   Later on, he found a correlation between the radiation spikes and unsolved crimes, especially violent crimes.   Then, about eighteen months ago, the police found a small fragment of brass gearing near a murder. They brought it to the college for metal analysis. It was soaked, I mean, absolutely *soaked* in this radiation.

Tommy watched her eyes, hoping she didn't notice the slight gasp that escaped his lips, and remembering that the guy had cried.   He remembered the murder well.

Dr. Liu continued. "I started thinking back to that geared spyglass. Why would anyone want something so badly broken? I tested the spyglass. It had way more than a normal amount of this radiation, like the fragment of brass.

I made a list of things that you and I had both bid on at auction. I then tested everything that we both went after that I won. Every piece was exposed to dark energy.   Now, my whole lab is soaked in that same radiation, my lab assistant is dead, and the police think I did it.   Quite honestly, Mr. White, I think you're the only one who can help me."

"Ok, let's assume for a second that you're not totally insane, and also that I believe you. I don't have anything to go on. Nowhere even to start."

"Well, I figured since you knew about these things, you would know who had them." Even with everything she had been through, she had been acting wrong. She was too guarded, too nervous. Eyes always on him. Tommy got it. She knew that he was aware of this energy, and she thought he might be involved with the people who trashed her lab, for all she knew; he could have been one of them.

"No. I don't know who did it, but I have noticed that things have changed around here in the past few months. Listen, let me think about it. Let me see what I can find out. Leave your card, and I'll let you know tomorrow if I'll help you.

"Thank you, Mr. White. I would appreciate any help you could give me. Money is no object."

"We'll talk about that later. As of now, I said I'll think about it."

"I understand."

"Right now, you should go home. The people who trashed your lab and killed your friend may not have found what they were looking for. Change up your routine. It could be the cops following you to try and get more evidence, or it could be whoever killed you friend. Either way, why make life any easier for them? Take some sick days, stay in at night. Watch your back, ok?"

She stood to leave. "Sick days won't be an issue, Mr. White. I'm on administrative leave until the case is settled."

"Jim, please, call me Jim."

"Ok, Jim. I'll be waiting for your call."

She stood and shook his hand. He could feel the damp in her palm. He thought about the risk she had taken coming to him, not knowing if he was involved, or even possibly the one who did it. She must be really desperate. Or stupid.

Tommy waited for her to leave then headed back upstairs. This case could lead him closer to the answers he was looking for, but it would put him in close contact with his favorite people, the Buffalo P.D. Closing the door to his little sanctuary, he did what he did every morning: he prayed for forgiveness.

He walked out the back door of his building. Today wasn't a day to drive. Dr. Liu had left his office a few hours ago, and he had spent the intervening hours trying to focus. He needed to walk today, to clear his mind, to get lost among the buildings.

Things had changed so much in this neighborhood over the years. He closed his eyes as he walked and remembered the way it used to be. So much activity, people and industry around here. Now, pretty much nothing. The street was empty. No one walked the streets anymore, not in this neighborhood. He could smell why he loved this place. Traveling around the world gives one perspective, but in all the places he had seen, there was nowhere that had that smell like a northeastern city. The metal, smoke, steam, gasses and particles in the air. It smelled like hard work. It always brought him back.

He scanned all around him, in window reflections, panning intersections with his eyes. There didn't seem to be anyone following him.

As he made his way downtown, the city was finally coming to life. Buses had started running, the trash men, early morning cleaning crews, the real heartbeat of a city. He could feel it, even in this place as he walked down Church Street past the Sheriff's office. Even in this sanitized governmental zone he could feel the rhythm of the town. Thump-thump, thump-thump. It had slowed since he first arrived so many years ago, but it still was beating. As he listened, he imagined he could hear it getting weaker. The city was dying, had been for close to thirty years now.

As he walked onto the campus, that strange post tragedy feeling was definitely there. Even though it had been weeks since the murder, the mood still lingered. It was paranoia. They say college is a community. Tommy always thought these places acted more like the small village he had grown up in. People hate each other, fight amongst themselves, spread rumors, all the normal human nastiness. But put an enemy at the gates, and suddenly they're a team, all for one and all that. Just like a village, it becomes an impenetrable wall to outsiders. No wonder the cops couldn't get anywhere.

There were still cops there, guarding the lab, he'd figured they would be. It usually takes them way too long to process a crime scene. That's mainly because they fumble around it so much that they have to triple-check everything. Of course, they looked for anything they could find. His search would be much more focused. He knew what to look for.

Tommy slipped under the crime scene tape and into the building. Some of the professors were milling around, but not many of them seemed to be doing actual work. He walked past the uniformed cops and assorted university staff. Experience had taught him that to blend in, the first thing he had to do was act like he belonged there, and rarely would anyone question his presence. Plus, with police in the building, the people who actually worked in the building probably felt safer than they should. In reality, stealing is made simpler by overconfidence in police presence.

Tommy found Dr. Liu's lab. Although any evidence would be hard to come by now. The place had been ransacked twice already; once by whoever broke in, and again by the police in their mad dash to blame it on the easiest suspect and get the case closed. He wasn't surprised to find the door missing. Usually the cops just take everything to their lab. Makes it easier to hide evidence that disagrees with them.

Dr. Liu was right: whoever broke in had completely trashed the place. The remains of computers and all sorts of other scientific instruments he didn't recognize lay scattered about the room. He stepped over a large, broken, flat panel display to gain entry. As he did, one of the detectives looked up from his notebook. The door, which had been knocked clear off its hinges, was leaning against a wall about ten feet into the room.

"White. Who let you in here?"

"You know me, Kowalski. I charmed my way in."

"Well, charm your happy ass right back out. This is an active crime scene, no civilians allowed." He loved to call Tommy a civilian. Thought it gave him authority.

"Actually, I'm working. I'm representing the rights of my client, Katrina Liu."

Kowalski rolled his eyes. He knew that if the girl's lawyer found out that the police wouldn't let an independent investigator look over the scene, it would look like they were hiding something to the jury. "Oh yeah? So you're representing our number one suspect. Looks like she's dumber than we thought."

"So you think she did all this damage? Honestly, Kowalski. I knew you were retarded, but I had no idea how serious it was." Tommy could see Detective Ted Kowalski's face getting redder, could hear the grinding of his teeth. He had a son with Down's Syndrome, and there was no word he hated more than *retarded*.

"Ok, funny guy. Who do you think it was?"

"Well, look at this door you've probably been staring at for three hours."

"What about it?"

"That's a steel security door. Steel hinges. High end."

"And?"

"Well, it probably weighs near a buck fifty. Dr. Liu might weigh what? One-ten? One Fifteen?"

"Maybe, why?" Kowalski's patience was getting thinner than his hair. The tone of his voice told Tommy to get to the point.

"Well, how did a hundred and ten pound woman knock a solid steel door off its hinges and halfway across the room, much less put a six inch dent in it?"

"I don't know, White, maybe she had an accomplice. Maybe it was you. You're decent sized guy. They got past security without being noticed, knew where the security cameras were, and nothing was taken. The way I see it, she was on thin ice with this pet project of hers." Kowalski tapped the tip of his pen against his little notepad, thinking through his words before he spoke. "The Dean already told me that he expected results, and soon. I say that she knew she wasn't going to get any, so she trashed her lab so that no one could tell that her work was pointless. There was a lot of money riding on this, White. Big time grants. If she didn't get some results soon, they were gonna cut it off and shut her down."

"What about the dead kid? Why would she kill her own lab assistant?"

"Cleaning up. She knew that he could rat on her trashing the lab and destroying the evidence of her failure, so she bumped him off."

"Makes sense to me, Kowalski. Even so, she's paying me to be here, so mind if I take a look around?"

"Yes, I do mind. I mind a whole hell of a lot, actually. You have five minutes, White. And don't touch anything. This is a *police* investigation, not some slob humping his neighbor's wife."

Tommy looked around. The place really was trashed. Monitors thrown on the floor, papers and shelving everywhere. That fucking fingerprint dust on everything. The more he looked around, the more Tommy knew that little Asian girl couldn't have done this. This damage would've taken a *very* strong man, no way someone her size could have thrown such heavy equipment. And it *was* thrown. One unidentifiable computer-looking box had taken out a chunk of drywall at head height before smashing on the floor. It looked like it weighed a hundred pounds.

Something caught Tommy's eye. He made his way through the trash to the other side of the room.

"Hey Kowalski."

The pudgy cop shuffled over. "You got two minutes left, White"

"How was the assistant killed?"

"M.E. says it was blunt force trauma."

"Ok. Tell me this, then. If you were a young, small woman with a gun, why would you beat a man who was much larger than you rather than just shoot him?"

"She didn't have a gun."

"Then explain to me where this bullet hole came from?" Tommy pointed to the computer tower on the floor in front of him on the floor. There was a hole in it surrounded by burned residue. Obviously gunpowder.

"Oh, goddamn it!" Kowalski yelled over his shoulder. "Hey, you! Yeah, come here."

A young man in a Crime Scene jumpsuit rushed over.

"How did you miss this?" Kowalski pointed at the bullet hole in the computer.

"I was processing the other side of the room, sir. I haven't been over here."

"How did everyone else miss it? Never mind. Just figure it out. Find out who missed this." Kowalski was like most cops: a mostly useless bully. He turned his anger on Tommy. "And you. Your time is up. Get out of my crime scene."

"Does being completely wrong ever get old for you, Kowalski? I guess not, or your lazy ass would just retire." Tommy stood to leave, pulling his watch from his pocket. He could feel it ticking through the case. "I have real work to do anyway. Your monkeys already fucked this scene up. Try not to lose the body, or that bullet hole. I know how you guys like to lose evidence." Tommy strode from the room.

Chapter 2

No matter how hard you try to hide a crime, no matter how careful you are, no matter what steps you take, someone always finds out. There are people in the world, people we pass by every day, that we never see. They are invisible. Waitresses, garbage men, janitors and bums on the sidewalk. They all have stories. They know everything that's important. Invisible people know invisible things.

That's what brought Tommy to Scotty's place. It wasn't anything special, but it wasn't bad, either: an average lower middle class house in South Buffalo, real close to West Seneca. He knocked on the back door. Living in one place long enough, you learn the local etiquette. Tommy knew that only salesmen and the cops go to the front door. After a minute, the inside door opened.

"Jim White. I don't want nothing to do with you, man."

"Come on, Scotty."

"No way. Last time I helped you out, I had cops outside my house for a month. I told you no more then, and I meant it."

"No cops this time, Scotty. I swear. Just need some information."

"That's what you said last time, Jim. Next thing I know, po po's at my door asking if I know anything about a murder. I can't get a murder rap, Jim. I already got two strikes."

"I'll make it worth your while, Scotty." Tommy held up a roll of bills. Scotty's face softened.

"How much?"

"Three now, another three if what you have pans out."

"You still owe me five from last time."

"Fine, plus that. But you know I don't carry a wad that big." Scottie opened the outside door.

"Get in here before someone sees you."

Tommy took a seat in the living room. Newspapers were stacked all around, mixed with accounting books and various types of notebooks. He had never been in Scotty's house before. It looked completely different from what he expected.

"You're starting to look old, Scott."

"You're not, Jim. Still look the same as the day we met."

Tommy examined the man across from him. His graying beard was untrimmed, skin sun baked to a darker shade than his normal mocha complexion.

"Good genes, I guess. How long's it been?"

"Six years."

"You're still playing the market?"

"And my fellow man, of course." Scotty was one of those street guys who talked to himself, shook his cup and hoped you'd drop something in out of fear or pity. It was a total scam. He had a college degree and had been an accountant before the mill he worked for closed in '81. Now he day traded from computers with money he earned pan handling.

"So, let's get to business." Scotty's voice was rougher than Tommy remembered.

"There was a murder."

"Damn it, man. I knew it. Don't you drag me into your shit again, Jim, I swear to God."

"No, Scotty, I didn't do it, I'm investigating it. Young kid was killed on campus. They're trying to pin it on the doctor he worked for there. I'm working for her. You know anything about it?"

"Just what I heard on the news. A few extra bills might jog me, though."

"Come on, Scott. You and I both know some seriously strange shit has been going on the past few months."

"Okay, okay. Yeah, I hear things. Little things, you know? Some of the street guys are moving up. Pushers moving off the street, bums getting apartments on the north side. Things that don't make sense. People saying there's a new heavy mover in town. Guy's throwing big bills around. Nobody knows who it is, though."

"Mafia? Irish?"

"Nah. I know most of those guys. Most of them from thirty years ago are still around. This guy's totally new, a real out of towner. I heard a rumor he's Russian."

"Russian mob?"

"Don't know, could be."

"You heard this new player was behind the campus break in?"

"Not in so many words, but that's the rumor."

"Rumors don't serve me, Scotty."

"Well, here's some facts for you then. From what I hear on the street, these guys come to you, and if you say no, you disappear. You say yes, they set you up good, like, real good, Jimmy."

"Who are they recruiting?"

"Can't really say. No one I know personally."

"Could you find out?"

"Well, that would depend..."

"Yeah, I know. I'm good for it."

"You better be this time, and with danger pay."

"Danger pay? Seriously?"

"Didn't you hear me the first time? If you say no, you disappear. I don't think this guy wants people asking a whole lot of questions. I'll need double, up front."

"A grand? Come on, Scotty."

"Yeah. A grand. Cash on hand. And by cash I mean bills. And by on hand, I mean mine, before I do shit."

"Fine." Tommy pulled his billfold out and counted out ten hundreds.

"You still owe me."

Tommy counted out another ten. "We're square now, Scotty. And I swear, you con me and you'll see me again. He pulled out a pen and scribbled a phone number on the front page of a newspaper. "Contact me here when you have something. And don't take your time, Scotty." Tommy walked toward the door. Scotty was already recounting the money.

"Nice to see you again, Scott."

"You too. 'I don't carry that big a wad.' Lying ass."

The walk home from Indian Church was cold. It was still early September, but that wicked, frosty winter wind had already started making its presence known almost as a warning that colder days were coming.

Tommy considered the facts: A) His pocket watch started ticking for the first time in years when he checked it in the lab. The place was soaked with energy. B) There weren't many things that could do the kind of damage he saw in that room. He could think of a few, but none of them had been seen in decades. C) Someone had made sure that every piece of recording equipment had been destroyed, even going as far as shooting hard drives. Plus, what Scotty had been hearing on the street was even more disturbing. Buffalo isn't the kind of town crime really tries to make inroads into. Drugs, maybe, being on the border, but old school organized crime? Those guys gave up on making money in this city in the seventies.

Tommy crossed over Buffalo Creek headed toward Bailey Avenue. As he walked, he looked around this very old part of town. It hadn't changed much in the years he'd been here. Large stretches of Seneca were still lined with the old two-story working class homes that the mills had built for their employees in the thirties. Great old houses, every one the same, just painted different muted colors.

He was almost at Babcock Street when that feeling hit him. He hadn't felt it in years. There was someone watching him, walking behind him. He couldn't quite get a look over his shoulder, but as many years as he had been a wanted man, he knew the feelings of paranoia were usually accurate. First inclination is run. It always is. But he couldn't do it this time. There was a good chance that whoever was following him knew something about the case, maybe even who had the device. They must've seen him at the lab and followed him to Scotty's.

This was a pretty decent part of the city, all things considered. That meant no help if things got ugly. There was a time when people around here would call the police and lock their doors to make sure the rabble didn't wander up to their door and bleed on the carpet waiting for the ambulance. Now they kept their doors locked and their mouths shut. It was too dangerous not to. Why the hell didn't he drive today?

Tommy turned a corner and pressed himself up against the side of the Seneca Deli. He heard the footsteps coming. They sounded heavy, really heavy. Steps that loud could belong to a man strong enough to knock a steel door off its hinges. He reached in his coat and fingered the butt of his pistol. People wouldn't get involved, but they *would* call the cops if someone started shooting.

Could he risk it here? Daylight? Public? He'd have to chance it. As long as he didn't kill the guy, it would probably be alright. He pulled a pistol from its holster. The footsteps reached the corner. Tommy stepped into the sidewalk and aimed the gun where he figured the head would be. He was wrong. By about a foot.

Tommy McKinney wasn't a small man by any standard. He stood around five foot ten and a solid buck-eighty. He figured he was in remarkable shape for a man his age. But the wall in front of him was closer to seven feet than six, and seemingly just as wide, and smiling.

"Damn, you're a big 'un, ain't you?"

"You gonna use that, Mr. White?"

"Not if I don't have to."

"I wouldn't if I were you, Mr. White. This is a peaceful neighborhood. Hate for the fine folks of Seneca Street to call the police over a little... discussion."

"Why are you following me?"

"Doin' my job, Mr. White. Need to know what you know about that murder."

"I know you're big enough to have done it." Tommy looked him over. "Also figure you're not the gun type. That means you have a little buddy, Big 'Un."

"My boss really thinks that the two of you should have a talk."

"Really?"

"Really."

Tommy cocked the hammer on the revolver.

"I'm not really in a talking mood right now."

"Well, boss said 'Bring him', so I'm bringing you."

The big man reached for Tommy's gun hand. Tommy did the one thing he could: He kicked Big 'Un in the balls.

The man fell with a small yelp. Tommy smacked the back of the huge head with his pistol, grabbing Big 'Un by the collar. Now he was in the shit. He just pulled a gun on this guy on a public street, beat him with it, and now there was nowhere to hide him. Tommy looked around. No alleys, nothing. He dragged the man to the only cover around: an empty lot with a white bison statue and a sign in the middle of it.

"You got the drop. Doesn't happen often." The big man mumbled.

"Who is it? Who's behind this?" Tommy kept the pistol leveled on the slumped monster as he went through his pockets.

"I don't know his name. We call him 'Boss.'"

"And what does your boss want with a physicist? Why did he try to destroy the girl's research?"

"Don't know. Wouldn't tell you if I did."

"Fair enough." Tommy leveled the pistol at the big man's crotch. "You don't seem to have much use for that massive skull of yours, but I bet you're partial to the little head, aren't you?" Tommy pulled something out of the man's inside coat pocket.

"Oh, what's this?" Tommy examined the tiny pin. It was gold, with some sort of Cyrillic writing around the edges. "Looks like a crest. Don't look too happy that I found it. Gift from your boss? Bet it is."

"I told you, I don't know. And I wouldn't tell you if I did."

"Yeah, that's too bad for you. When you wake up, go tell your boss that if he wants to see me, he can come get me himself." Tommy watched a group of young men walk by on the sidewalk, intentionally not looking back at him. Tommy slapped the butt of his gun against Big 'Un's jaw. He looked at the sign the man fell against.

"Welcome to the Seneca Babcock Community. Where Neighbors Care." He chuckled a bit.

As Big 'Un slumped unconscious against the sign, Tommy heard tires squeal on the street. There was that authoritative yell of a cop and the slamming of a car door. Tommy holstered the pistol and ran down an alley between two rows of houses. He didn't want to outshoot them, even though he could: He'd had years of practice.

Tommy stepped up on a trash can and vaulted the dividing fence into a driveway at the end of the alley. All that time training, learning the *ropes*, hours on the high wire and the trampoline. There was no way that two weighed-down beat cops would be able to clear that jump.

Tommy crossed Orlando Street in a couple steps. As he reached the other side, he looked back to see the first cop running toward him and the second just clearing the top on the wall. Who were these guys? He didn't think anyone could've made that jump like he did, certainly not some doughnut eater on government pay.

Tommy took off at a sprint. The first cop may have been agile, but the second was a dead sprinter. In just a few steps, he was at Tommy's heels, matching him step for step. Tommy was breathing hard, running up a street in broad daylight chased by two cops. The cop behind him wasn't even straining.

There was a hand on the back on his neck. Tommy went down hard on the sidewalk. In a heartbeat both cops were on him, nightsticks, boots and fists flying. He could take a punch, even a few kicks, but this was severe. These jokers weren't even giving him the normal "stop resisting" line as they kicked the hell out of him.

When they got bored, they cuffed him. Cop #1, the agile one, sat him on the sidewalk and watched him as cop #2, the fast one, ran back to get the car. After they had frisked him and pulled his guns and tactical batons, with the requisite rib-jabs and rough frisking (Tommy always thought there was something homoerotic about that part), they threw him in the back of the car.

There was none of the normal banter, no matter how much he taunted them. They didn't even call an ambulance for Big 'Un, just took Tommy downtown. He had been here before. There was a time when the cops wouldn't take a troublemaker to the station, just find a nice quiet alley to beat the shit out of you, and leave you with a warning. Those were the old days. Now you could sue the cops. This was a rare situation.

To his surprise, they pulled into Buffalo Police headquarters. They dragged him from the car directly into an interrogation room. He sat there alone, hands cuffed behind his back, sucking the blood out of his teeth in the big mirror. It seemed like hours. Tommy's vintage suit was trashed, seams torn, all grime and blood. Finally the door opened.

"Can't even get a mile from a crime scene without committing a crime yourself, can you, White?" Kowalski's attempt at an intimidating voice was almost laughable, if he hadn't had a cardboard box marked "evidence" in his hands. This was no warning visit.

"You know me, Kowalski. I'm a little retarded." Tommy smiled across the table at the obese detective, watching his face get redder. "You know what that's like, don't you? Being R-E-T-A-R-D-E-D?" Tommy spelled out the word nice and slow, accents on every letter.

"Think you're funny, do you? Well, I got you this time, White. See, I looked up Jim White when they brought you in. You're *not* Jim White. The Jim White you claim to be died in 1978 in Syracuse. I got his death certificate right here." Kowalski laid a photocopy of the document in front of Tommy. "Same Social Security number, same date of birth, everything. Except this kid died before he turned a year old. Your birth certificate? Yeah, I got that, too. It's a fake, and not a very good one. That hovel you live in is owned by something called Merrick & Co. Shady business, from what I can tell. For some reason, I can't seem to find the names of any of the owners of the company."

"So? I named my business after the company that originally owned the building. I'm sentimental like that." As Kowalski leaned forward, Tommy noticed a small gold tie tack the detective was wearing. It was the same as the pin he had taken off Big 'Un.

"Sounds more like a front to me, and then there's these." Kowalski reached into the evidence box and pulled out two bags: Tommy's revolvers. "Nice iron. Looks antique. Also, it seems you don't have a carry permit. It doesn't figure, though. You strike me as more of a Beretta kind of guy."

"No one worth giving a gun should need more than six shots. By the way, nice Glock."

Kowalski smirked at the comment. He was arrogant when he thought he had the upper hand. "So, what do you really know about the break in at the lab?"

"No more than you do, honestly. Other than the girl didn't do it."

"Well, my boss thinks you're a little more interested in this case than you should be."

"Send him on in. I'll tell him the same thing I'm telling you. Fuck off." Kowalski made a motion toward the camera in the corner of the room, then came across the table. The punch he threw knocked Tommy out of the chair onto his back.

"I'm sick of your mouth, White. Or whatever your name is. The girl's going down for the murder, and there's nothing you or anyone can do about it. And if you don't back off, you'll go down for it, too."

Tommy smelled wet peat in the air. He could hear rain falling all around him. He looked up at Kowalski, but saw the dark silhouette of a British officer standing in his place. He felt the blood on his face.

"I'll *make sure* the bullets we found in that lab match these guns. Yeah, I think she hired you to pull the trigger for her. Then you come back playing innocent and pretending to work the case on her behalf. Perfect reason for you to get into the crime scene and make sure you did all the damage you needed to. What are you laughing at?"

Tommy pushed himself to a standing position against the wall, a bloody smile spreading across his face. There were soldiers all around him now. Bayonets fixed, muskets pointed at him. He could hear his wife crying in the distance. He tried to look at Kowalski, but his vision had changed. Everything looked red. He fought to keep control.

"A few things, actually, Detective. First, you hit like a pussy."

Kowalski came around the table and slugged him again, knocking him back to the floor. Tommy stood himself back up. It was over. There would be blood. He saw that Redcoat officer's arrogant smile all over the Detective's face. Tommy could take his time now. Plan. Wait. Make it painful.

"Second, I'm thinking how your son would feel about knowing his dad is a dirty cop." The shot this time was in the gut. Tommy reacted more than he needed to, sliding part way down the wall.

Kowalski stepped forward. He was right in Tommy's face now. Nasty fast food breath and spittle spreading all over Tommy's face.

"Third: This is the second time today that someone's threatened me in the name of their 'Boss.' He had the same tie tack as you, too. Quite a coincidence, and..."

"And what?"

"You should never stand this close to a dangerous suspect." Tommy head butted the obese cop. He stumbled backward. Tommy braced himself against the wall and kicked out. His heel caught Kowalski in the middle of the chest. The detective fell backward. Tommy hopped in the air, pulling his cuffed hands under his feet to the front.

The cop took a swing. Tommy blocked it with his forearms, deflecting the blow to the right. He brought an elbow up into the Kowalski's chin. Grabbing the back of the detective's head, Tommy pulled it down, landing several hard knees to the face before throwing Kowalski across the room and crushing the table under his weight.

Tommy was back on him in a flash, slamming him face-first into the back wall of the room. Kowalski tried again to land a punch, this one to the stomach. Tommy brought the metal handcuffs down on the detective's wrist mid-swing, making him howl in pain. He grabbed the back of Kowalski's head and pushed him face-first into the large two-way mirror. The glass spider webbed from the impact. Tommy took two running steps on the wall to gain height, bringing a final knee into the still-standing cop's face.

Kowalski hit the floor dazed. Tommy went through his pockets, digging out the handcuff key. He kept his knee in the middle of the detective's back as he unlocked the cuffs and slapped them on Kowalski's wrists.

"I don't give a damn who you think I might be. Just know this: I'm very, very dangerous to you right now. We're going to walk out of here, and no one tries to stop me." Tommy pulled his things from the evidence box and dragged the cop to his feet.

He pressed the barrel of his revolver against Kowalski's head. "No heroics, fat man. Simple as that."

"You know that gun ain't loaded, White."

"I know, you know, they don't." Tommy squeezed the fingers of his right hand around Kowalski's throat at the Adam's Apple, then pulled open the door and started screaming.

"Guns down. On the floor. Now. Do it or I swear to God this fat pig dies."

Kowalski was trying to tell them it wasn't loaded, but Tommy's death grip around his vocal chords choked off his voice.

"Step back. Do it now. Clear the hall. Everyone at the end of the hall." Tommy watched the cops walk backward. Only one had actually put down his gun. The rest were trying to hide theirs. He didn't figure any of them would give it up, it was a long shot. He pushed Kowalski forward until he reached the pistol on the floor. Tommy had to let go of the fat cop's throat to reach the gun. Luckily his hostage was fat enough to cover his movements for the most part, but if Kowalski dropped now, Tommy would be caught out with nothing but an empty gun and a building full of angry cops.

Bobbing to the floor, he picked up the semi-automatic. Chambering a round, he heard a frustrated noise from his hostage.

"It wasn't loaded, you stupid fucks. The fucking gun was *unloaded*."

"Nice to see you keep with such intelligent company, boyo. I think I could have done that with a candy bar."

"Fuck you, White. You still have to get out of the building." Kowalski had trouble getting the words out; he was still dazed and had gashes all over his face and upper body from hitting the glass.

"Yeah. But I've been in this situation before, fat man." Tommy pulled Kowalski into an office off the main hall, keeping the detective between Tommy and the cops' guns.

"You cornered yourself, White. Third floor, straight to the ground. No way out."

"Third floor? Yes. Straight to the ground? Well, I suppose we'll see." Tommy shoved the bloodied Kowalski into the crowd of cops that had collected in the doorway, knocking them down like bowling pins.

Kowalski heard the window shatter. Fumbling to his feet, he ran to the hole and looked down, expecting to see White's body splayed out on the sidewalk. Nothing there. No body, nothing. Something made him turn right. What he saw made him sick to his stomach.

Jim White was running, not crawling, *running* along the five inch wide ledge three stories off the ground. As he watched, White reached the corner of the building and leapt across Franklin Street to the fire escape on the building opposite.

All the cops were staring, transfixed by the strange sight of a man now hurtling down the outside of an office building like a monkey dropping through tree limbs.

Tommy hit the ground harder than he had hoped. He knew he was banged up, but no time to wonder how badly now. His eyes darted around. No cops in sight, but they would be soon. Had to get off the street. Now. He flashed back to years before: The smell of gunpowder, screaming, shocked faces. The old city, the smog, smokestacks...

Snapping himself back to reality, Tommy bolted up the street several blocks before turning. He could hear the sirens coming quickly, and footsteps even closer. Then came the shots. The first one clipped the wall at head height as he turned a corner, spraying him with chunks of brick. The next was like fire in his right side, just below his ribs. Tommy chanced a glance behind him. It was cop #2 from this morning. Tommy knew he couldn't outrun him, not anymore. He pulled the gun he stole from the cop and fired two quick shots in the cop's general direction. The first hit a parked car, the second clipped the wall. Tommy couldn't waste bullets, and he couldn't win a foot race.

With the cop closing the thirty yard gap fast, he turned and dropped to one knee.

Cop #2 didn't try to dodge, Tommy fired twice more.

The first missed, passing through the man's shirt. The second hit square in the leg, making the man *pirouette*. The bullet made a strange metallic sound hitting the cop. Tommy turned and started to run again, this time zigzagging through alleys and backstreets until he got to an older section of downtown he knew well. Within blocks, the cop was back on him, seemingly unfazed by the bullet in his leg. This time, though, Tommy knew he could get away. Ducking through an old wooden gate, he came out in a narrow alley between two buildings. He knew this spot, knew its history, knew what was just below.

Squeezing into a small gap in the alley wall, Tommy felt the ancient wood of a stable door. He felt with his hand until his fingers touched the rusty iron latch. It moved hard, but it moved. The door fell open behind him, and he dropped down a flight of stairs into darkness.

The heavy footsteps of the cop passed by in the alley above. Tommy waited until he couldn't hear them anymore and felt his way back up the stairs to shut the door. As the old latch dropped back into place, he smiled. No one remembered this place. Once, this building was alone on the block, a livery stable. As the city grew, zoning laws changed, and they built another building almost literally on top of it. In fact, the upper floors are connected, but this coal cellar, with its door nearly blocked off by the other building, was completely forgotten since Prohibition, when they used it to hide booze after it came across the frozen lake in winter. There was even a tunnel leading out. At least there used to be. It had been years.

Chapter 3

The leaking foundation had stained the stones with calcium and other minerals. It had begun to crack since the last time he was here. Some stones were out of place on the floor, others were mostly rotted away. He fumbled about in the darkness, wishing that he had kept a flashlight in his coat, or at least a lighter. He wondered for a moment if quitting smoking had been a mistake. Actually, he wondered that a lot. Maybe old age really was getting to him. Had he been a younger man, would he have remembered where the tunnel entrance was? The gate led to several miles of tunnels opening onto other abandoned sub basements in other ancient buildings all over the city and beyond its limits. His escape from Buffalo.

He had thought many times about this tunnel over the years: There were rumors in the old days that it had been a part of the Underground Railroad. It would make sense. The bricks were that old at least. As with most places that have multiple purposes over the years, there was probably a totally mundane reason for its original construction. A drainage tunnel or something. It didn't really matter at this point, but he often wondered about things that were older than him.

Tommy dug through the layers of trash and debris and scum that had collected throughout the decades where he thought the tunnel might be. He fought the pain in his side, trying to ignore the pain, that stomach full of dread one gets when something is *really* wrong, the feeling of blood draining from his body. There was nothing he could do about it right now. Here in the dark, the only option he had was to get to somewhere safer. He had to get to Dr. Liu. She was in danger and didn't even know it yet. If something happened to her now, he might never get the

~ 48 ~

information she had; never get closer to the answers he was looking for. He only really had one place to go; now all he had to do was get there.

There it was. He felt the edge of one of the iron hinges that held the false brick door. Walking his fingers around the seam, he found the small rusted pin opposite the hinges. The pin didn't want to go easily. Probably hadn't moved since the forties. After fifteen minutes of wrenching and twisting, the pin moved. Even drenched in sweat, he could feel the warm blood still running free from the wound in his side and now from his torn fingertips.

He took a deep breath, bracing himself against the coming pain, and slammed his shoulder into the door. It moved slightly. Another shot, gritting his teeth against the pain, and the door broke free. Now came the hard part. This door led to an unlit and uncharted labyrinth of tunnels leading to blocked off doors all over downtown and beyond. Probably fifteen miles of tunnels. He had to feel the wall for the marks left by the bootleggers. If he lost his way or missed a mark, an unseen drop could kill him, or worse, he might spend eternity trying to find his way out.

The walls of the tunnel were covered in slime. Ages had passed since anyone had come this way, and it showed. Even in his day, the tunnels were disgusting and partially filled in with every indescribable type of detritus, now they were nearly impassable. Tommy felt the stones for the first mark. He knew it was about a foot past the entrance, but since the whole tunnel was coated with something living, now he couldn't make out the rough carved edges of the arrows.

Finally he felt something. It was faint, but as he read it with his fingers he knew the shape: A resting cross. A mark he had used many times himself to indicate a safe place. It was one of the many things that criminals of the past had borrowed from the gypsies of Europe. It pointed down the tunnel. There would be another on the left facing the opposite way at the first junction. His body was hunched over in a crouching position as Tommy shuffled along the edge of the tunnel, trying to stay off the bottom.

There was a very particular smell in this place: Decay, moisture, mixed with the bacterial stench of a broken sewer pipe on a hot day. Even in his own situation he couldn't help but think about the escaped slaves who had used this tunnel as a place to hide while passage to Canada was arranged for them. Days, possibly weeks down here in the indefinable muck and stink. He pushed the thoughts from his head. Now these tunnels had a different kind of fugitive to shelter.

One not nearly so innocent or deserving of freedom. He staggered along with one hand on the wall, the other trying to staunch the blood flowing from his side.

He had travelled for what had to be miles in the tunnels, having to stop several times to vomit or catch his breath against the smell, like rotten eggs and shit, that permeated the walls and arched ceiling. The vomiting sent bolts of pain through him, but Tommy knew from experience that it was the pain that was keeping him from going into shock. Soon he saw a sliver of faint light several yards away. He moved toward it slowly.

He approached the doorway, giving his eyes time to adjust to the brightness of what appeared to be sunlight. The door was unblocked. That was good. There was a different smell in the air now. A comparative freshness to the vileness of the tunnel. Tommy hoped he went the right way. He hoped he had remembered what he had tried to memorize so long ago.

Crawling on his hands and knees to the small door, he peeked through a crack in the ancient wood. A basement. Unfinished. Rough stone walls. This was the place.

The house on Clark Street. So many memories here. The first place he stayed. That was so many names ago. It was pretty much a shit hole now, but he was thankful he had held on to it.

Tommy pushed the tunnel door open and hopped down into the basement. Everything down here seemed exactly as he left it. His medical books, a decent military medic's kit. Not much, but enough to keep him from dying.

He flipped on the exam light and sat on the small table. Peeling off his shirt, he examined the hole in his side. It was caked with congealed blood, but there was still some flowing from the wound. The shot went right through, but it didn't seem to have hit anything major.

Now he had to see to his hand. Two of the fingers on his right hand were bent at odd angles. He gritted his teeth and slotted them back in place, taping them together with a metal splint on each. He cleaned the small cuts on his left hand with peroxide and sealed them with Super Glue.

He cleaned the bullet wound in his side as best he could, scrubbing it out with saline solution before sewing it with medical sutures, the whole time choking back screams.

No one could know anyone was here. He had been very careful with this place, keeping it in just good enough condition to make sure it wasn't torn down, but bad enough that it looked abandoned.

His knee was swelling. He could feel it through his trousers. Tommy stripped to his boxers and saw an immediate problem: His right kneecap was shifted almost completely to the outside.

He had to act quickly, before the swelling made it any harder to fix. He pulled an ace bandage from the medical kit and grabbed a handful of tongue depressors. Biting down on the bits of wood, Tommy forced his kneecap back into place. He screamed through his teeth, tears streaming from his eyes. He quickly wrapped his knee as tightly as he could with the ace bandage, his vision getting grayer with each passing moment.

Tommy awoke on the cold metal exam table the next morning. As he tried to move, his memory of the previous day and night came rushing back in an orgy of pain.

He had wrapped an ice pack on his knee before he passed out, and the swelling there seemed under control. While changing the bandage on the bullet wound, he noticed a bit of an infection forming, but he knew that wouldn't kill him.

He couldn't put weight on the leg yet, that would take a while. He just hoped it would happen eventually. He hopped up the stairs and into the kitchen of the house.

Everything here was pretty much how he had left it, too, if covered in a bit more dust than he remembered. There was enough canned food for a few months and kerosene to heat and cook with for the same amount of time. The power was still on.

Tommy struggled upstairs. There was one bedroom, the other two having been converted when he bought the place. He had put weeks into it. Everything was covered in sheets now, but his bookshelves were still in place in the library. He left the other room locked for the time being, he would get to that soon enough.

For now, though, he had to think about Katrina. She was in more trouble than she knew. This was no normal murder. There was a bigger goal for whoever was framing her, and it looked like the police, or at least Detective Kowalski and those two uniformed cops, were in on it. He had to figure some way to get her to safety if he could.

He also had to figure out who this new boss was. Strange things were happening in Buffalo again. He couldn't say it was just like before, but it was damn sure too familiar to ignore. The devices, the strange crimes, people disappearing and being attacked. The darkness was coming back to the Nickel City on the winter wind. Tommy had a sick feeling in his stomach.

He hobbled down the hall to the locked room. Fishing out his keys, he opened the three deadbolts and flicked on the light switch. The room was bathed in a pale fluorescence. Sitting down at a small desk, he powered up a computer. While it was loading, he checked the status of three cell phones that sat on chargers on one corner of the desk. Burn phones. Enough minutes on them to make a couple of short calls or check messages. Once the computer finished powering up, Tommy started checking the local news for information on his escape from police custody.

There was a surprising lack of coverage. Just a short piece about a suspect escaping from police custody with his license photo and the name Jim White. Nothing about the running gunfight with the two cops, nothing about the murder. Kowalski must have kept the real reason he was in custody quiet. That meant that the rest of the police probably weren't involved. As much as Tommy hated the cops, most of them were honest, if a bit simple. They had a sense of honor, even if it included occasionally fabricating evidence. But most important, they hated being made fools of. If they knew that Kowalski was playing them, they'd never stand for it.

One of the burn phones rang. It was the number he had given to Scotty. Tommy answered.

"Hello?"

"Jim? What the hell, man? What have you gotten me into?"

"Scotty. Relax. This isn't what it looks like."

"It never is with you, is it? You're wanted, man. You know that, right?"

"Yeah, I know. It's a setup, Scotty."

"I figured that. Man, every time I see you. Every time!"

"I'm sorry, Scott. I really am. Listen, have you managed to find anything out?"

"Yeah, but listen, man. We can't talk about this on the phone. I gotta meet you somewhere." Shit. If Scotty was working with the cops, he'd lead them right to him. If he said no, Scotty would take off with whatever information he had.

"Okay. I'm hiding out. I'm out in Fillmore. Come out this way. Call this number when you get close."

"Got it man, I'll be there in half an hour. After this, I'm done. I can't help you anymore on this one, Jimmy. This is some weird, scary shit."

"I got you, Scotty." Tommy hung up the phone. He had half an hour to get ready for a siege.

He hopped back down to the basement and got his pistols from where he had taken them off last night. Then, climbing back up the stairs, he went to the computer room and opened the closet door. Inside were several trunks. He opened the top one and pulled out a small chest. He grabbed two boxes of ammunition and a couple of tactical knives and collapsible batons. Pulling a gun cleaning kit out of the trunk, he went back to the desk.

It only took him a few minutes to give the revolvers a once-over and a reload. He went into the bedroom and pulled a fresh shirt, vest, and pants out of vacuum bags in the closet. After redressing, he strapped his pistols in their shoulder holsters and the batons and knives to his belt and went back to the computer room to watch the wifi based security cameras for Scotty and any unusual police presence.

Not long after he sat down, the phone rang again.

"Scotty."

"Yeah, it's me, Jim."

"Were you followed?"

"Don't think so."

"Okay. Corner of Clark and Paderewski. Sign says Troy's Upholstering. Go around back."

"Gotcha. Be there in a few."

Tommy went down to the backdoor. It was the only outside entrance that wasn't barricaded on the building. He pulled a kitchen chair up next to the door, pulled out his pistols, and waited.

After a few minutes there was a knock at the door. Tommy waited, listening. He strained to hear voices, extra feet on the stairs, anything that might indicate that Scotty wasn't alone. Scotty knocked again.

"Come on, Jim. You really want me waiting on the steps?" Tommy slid the curtain aside. There stood Scotty, in all his bum glory, all alone. Tommy holstered his pistols and opened the door.

"Jesus, Scotty. Dressed like that people will call the cops for a suspicious vagrant." Scotty stepped inside. Tommy shut and locked the door behind him.

"Yeah," Scotty pulled at the lapel of his tattered jacket. "I figured people wouldn't notice me as much dressed like this."

Tommy chuckled. "You're probably right. Showing up on this street in your Brooks Brothers, people would think you were trying to buy the place."

"Hey. This is Brooks Brothers. Besides, you don't exactly blend here either, white boy."

"I don't go outside. Okay, Scotty. Have a seat. You want coffee or tea?" Scotty sat at the kitchen table.

"Tea, if you don't mind."

Tommy started the kettle and sat down.

"So this is what I found out. This guy, I can't get a name on him. He's recruiting heavily among the street people. I mean heavily." Scotty said.

"Who's he recruiting?"

"That's the thing. He's not just taking anybody. Mostly they're ex military, some educated people, too. He's pulling all the people with brains off the street."

"Did you get a description?"

"Of the man himself, no. But the guy who goes out on the street, in person, that's a different story."

"So who is he?"

"No name, but the guys call him 'the Russian'. Now, I'm not getting this info from particularly smart guys, Jimmy. Mostly the drunks he didn't ask."

"What are they saying about him?"

"They say he has a thick accent, about six foot, old, worn suits. Hair combed to the side. He wears old style tinted granny glasses, carries himself like he's been to school. One of the bums called him 'The Aristocrat'; he's got a nasty scar on his forehead. Always carries a bunch of cash. They say there's something creepy about him."

"What's that?"

"Well, one of the guys I talked to was in Afghanistan. He said this guy looked like the suicide bombers he saw over there. That weird stare. You know what I mean?"

"Yeah, I know it. A true believer." The kettle whistled. Tommy got up and steeped the tea.

"Yeah, that's the type."

"The guy's a religious freak." Tommy stared at the teapot on the stove. If this guy was who he thought it was, "freak" barely touched it.

"Yeah. Seems that way. You know these guys? They Muslims?"

Tommy handed Scott a cup. Scott took a long, slow sip.

Tommy looked at his tea. "No, not Muslims. They're something much more dangerous than Jihadists." They sat in silence for a few minutes, each sipping from their cup.

"Well, you better get out of here."

"Yeah, I better. Don't want to be out in this neighborhood after dark. Some unsavory characters around here." Scotty set down his cup then looked down at his clothes and smiled. He got up and headed toward the door. "Hey Jim, there's something I've been meaning to ask you."

"What's that?"

"How long we known each other?"

"Maybe twenty years. Why?"

"Well, in all that time. You look the same. No grey hairs, no lines on your face, nothing. How is that?"

Scotty was staring him down. Tommy could feel it. He was searching Tommy's face, looking for an answer.

"I suppose I'll just call it a blessing and a curse."

"Yeah, sure." Scotty didn't believe him. He knew there was more to it, but he wasn't asking. That was the Buffalo way. Tommy had trusted it for years to protect himself.

"I wish I could tell you more, Scott. One day I will, but this isn't the time."

"Yeah, I got you." Scott walked over to the door.

"Hey Scotty?"

"Yeah?"

"I got a favor to ask you."

"What do you need now?" Scotty was being cautious. Tommy really couldn't blame him.

"I need you to contact someone for me, give him this message." Tommy wrote a quick note on a pad he kept on the counter. Scotty looked it over and handed it back to him. "Can I trust you to do that?"

"Yeah. I got you. But this one's a little weird, even for you."

"One more thing, Scotty. You might want to keep your head down for a while. I think this new guy in town is pretty heavily connected. He's got cops on the payroll."

"Who doesn't?"

"Seriously, Scott. Stay off the street until this is over. Whoever these guys are, they're willing to kill in public to protect their plan."

"I hear you, Jim. You just can't seem to stay out of trouble, can you?"

"It's a gift. Take care of yourself."

"You too, Jim." Scotty stepped through the door and disappeared into the growing darkness.

Tommy shut and locked the door and limped upstairs. His knee was healing well, but it would still be a few days before he would be able to handle himself on the street again.

He made his way to the library. Pulling the sheet off a cabinet, he dug through ancient looking notebooks. Something about Scotty's description of the Aristocrat tripped a memory. That description, he knew that description. There were hundreds of notebooks, spanning decades.

There it was. A notebook full of photos. Flipping through, page after page after page of yellowing images. Long dead faces staring back at him. None of them smiling, but staring with a kind of derision he recognized. Anyone who grew up poor knew that look. He flipped another page and there it was.

An early photograph of ladies and gentlemen. The men were standing behind the women who were seated in plush chairs. Maybe fifteen people in all. All of them dressed in nineteenth century finery, except one.

He stood in the middle of the image, a long scraggly beard flowing over his black robes. Two fingers of his right hand raised over his chest, caught in the motion of making the sign of the cross. He was tall compared to the other men, heavily set, and with long hair parted in the middle and plastered to his head. He was Grigori Rasputin, and the man who stood immediately to his right was tall and wearing shaded granny glasses.

Tommy looked to the margin at the bottom of the image. In rough script were the names of the attendees of this party in St. Petersburg, capital of Tsarist Russia. Next to the name Rasputin he found his answer: Vladimir Grozny. He didn't have the scar in this picture, but Tommy knew it was him.

He was thrown. Grozny was supposed to have died with the rest of the Russian royal family in the revolution that overthrew the Tsar fifteen years after this picture had been taken. Now, apparently this long-dead man was recruiting for his cult in Buffalo. If Tommy was right, this was bad. Really really bad.

It was time. Tommy couldn't hide anymore. He had to get out and find out what Grozny was doing in Buffalo. He had to be a detective again. In the morning, before the sun came up, he would go get his car and find Grozny. Everything was starting to make sense, and Katrina was in greater danger than he had thought.

Chapter 4

Katrina Liu was watching *The Matrix* for the eighth time when her doorbell rang. She looked at the clock: 10:45. She had already talked to her lawyer earlier today, and didn't expect to hear from him for another two weeks at least. The knock came again, this time more insistent. It could be the detective, Jim White. She had given him her address. But he also had her phone number. Wouldn't it make more sense to call if he had information?

She walked over to the window. There was a youngish looking man in unstylish street clothes on her stoop. His old Corolla was double parked, and he seemed to be alone. What could he possibly want? She walked downstairs and opened the door without unhooking the chain.

"Can I help you?"

"Dr. Katrina Liu?"

"Yes. What can I do for you?" He couldn't be more than twenty-two.

"I'm here on behalf of Jim White, the detective you hired. He needs you to come with me." The young man looked up and down the street. His eyes were wide open and his pupils were dilated.

"Why couldn't he come himself, if it's so important?" Katrina instinctively pressed her foot against the back of the door, wedging her shoe between the door and the hardwood floor.

"He's been injured, ma'am. He sent me to bring you somewhere safe. Please, we don't have much time. We believe that your life is in danger." The man gestured, and a string rosary slipped out of his sleeve around his left wrist.

"Who are you?"

"My name is Michael. I work at Our Lady of Victory Basilica. Mr. White is a friend of the church." His voice had a strange southern twang, with what seemed like a touch of French mixed in.

"He didn't seem like the type."

"Apparently Mr. White is a very complex man. But there's no time to explain now. We have reason to believe that some police officers are involved in the murder of your assistant and the attempted murder of Mr. White. Now please, ma'am. Get your things. You're not safe here."

"What do you mean I'm not safe? The cops have been watching me day and night. How much more protection do I need?"

"The police are watching you? Right now?"

Katrina nodded. "Then we have to go. Please Dr. Liu. We have to go now." The young man looked desperate. Panic swept across his face. Katrina saw movement beyond him on the street.

Two uniformed cops were running across the street toward her door. They had their guns drawn. Katrina saw the look in their eyes. She saw anger. They weren't acting like police. One of them raised his gun and fired a shot toward the door. It struck the wall next to the door frame. There was no time to think. She released the chain on the door and let the young man in.

The door had barely shut before the cops were banging on it. Katrina locked both the deadbolt and the chain. They kept insisting that she open it while Michael just stared at the inside of the door, frozen. Their threats quickly went from arrest to death. They were shouldering the door now, trying to get in.

She ran to the back door and looked through the blinds: There was no one out there. No one she could see, anyway. Running back to the front room she saw Michael with his shoulder against the door as it bounced in a little further every time they hit it. The men outside had broken the lock. Now the only thing holding it was an ancient chain lock and a young holy man who looked like he was ready to piss himself. Every time the door pushed in, she could see their faces. Twisted, horrible mad faces. Barely human. They looked like the addicts she had seen at the shelter where she did her semester of community work. Hollow, broken, barely human faces.

She grabbed a fireplace poker. It was all she could find to defend herself. These were *not* normal police. They didn't want to arrest her. She could hear it in their voices. Michael was right. She was in real danger.

The door popped open again. She jabbed through the gap with the poker. It hit the cop in the chest and glanced to the side. He let out a howl as the door slammed shut. Michael was pointing behind her. She looked where he indicated. In the side window was another horrible face. The second cop must have let off the door and circled around to find another way in. She spun around and smashed the window with the poker. The hook caught the cop across the face. His head snapped to the side. Grabbing the poker, he ripped it from her hand and threw it aside. He was trying to crawl in the window. Katrina screamed and grabbed the closest thing she could, the iron ash shovel that went with the fireplace set. She hit the cop over and over, in the head, in the shoulders, anywhere she could swing. Finally he gave up trying to come through the tiny window and disappeared.

Michael was losing the fight to hold the door shut. Every time the door bounced in, he slid back a little further. Soon he would be pushed in, or the door would come right off its hinges.

As Katrina looked at Michael, his face changed somehow. The look on his face went from fear to a kind of understanding. He was whispering to himself. Praying. He seemed to be waiting for something. The pressure on the door slacked for a moment. Michael stepped clear. When the cop slammed into it again, he went straight through. Apparently unprepared, the man careened across the room and landed hard on the floor. Michael was on him in less than the blink of an eye. There was a fierceness in him that she didn't anticipate. He started kicking the downed man over and over again in the head. Blood flowed from the cop's mouth and nose. His face was covered in bleeding gashes from Michael's boots. Katrina could hear bones cracking from across the room. The man's nose made a strange wet sound as the boot made contact. There was a final loud crack of bone. The cop's jaw shifted to a horrible angle. Michael stopped kicking as the cop's head struck the floor. Katrina ran to the door just as the second cop cleared the threshold. She swung the shovel hard and this time pegged him square in the side of the head. He dropped where he stood.

Michael grabbed Katrina's hand. He had tears in his eyes.

"I don't think they're dead. Grab whatever you need quickly. We have to go right now."

Katrina grabbed her coat, wallet, and cell phone. He led her out the door and down to his car. The cops must not have noticed it running in front of the building.

Sweat poured from Michael's face as he jumped in the driver's seat and gunned the engine, barely giving Katrina time to shut her door. As they pulled away they heard the sirens wailing up the street behind them. Michael slammed the pedal into the floorboards so hard Katrina heard it. The little car wailed complaints as he pushed it beyond its limits. Tires screamed and smoked with every turn and lane change. The smell of overheated oil and burned rubber filled the cabin. His face was stony as he spun the little beater through the narrow city streets. The larger police cars had to slow for the turns, but even so they were gaining ground.

They were in downtown now. The streets were wider here, giving the more powerful cop cars a chance to catch up. Katrina was holding on to the door and dashboard to keep from being thrown into the young man's lap. Michael downshifted hard. The engine bounced off the rev limiter as he pulled the parking brake. Throwing the wheel to the left, he aimed the car for a narrow alley. There was a grinding of metal and sparks on Katrina's side of the car. The back of the car bounced off the alley wall. Michael corrected. There was no room to slide in the alley. Sparks flew from both sides of the car. Both mirrors were gone. He made another handbrake turn out of the alley. There was more traffic on this street, but still Michael showed no sign of slowing. He ran straight through red lights. The lights were timed to thirty miles per hour. They were doing closer to eighty.

Up ahead there were more flashing lights. A roadblock. Michael skidded to a stop in the middle of the road. He lowered his head for a moment before staring out at the roadblock and the police with drawn guns waiting for them.

Michael shifted his eyes to her. "How badly do you want to live?"

Katrina stared at him. She felt sick. She tasted nickel. She was gripping the car so hard she couldn't feel her hands.

"I suppose that's a good answer."

Michael dumped the clutch. The small tires spun for a moment before catching traction. The little car that had been through so much sprang forward. They were headed straight into the roadblock. Katrina knew she was screaming. Her mouth was open. She could feel the breath moving through her throat. She couldn't hear it.

The car cleared the two hundred yard gap in seconds. At a hundred feet strange spider webs started appearing on the windshield. There were flashes from the roadblock. Michael pushed Katrina under the dashboard.

Michael waited until the last possible moment. He threw his body and the wheel to the right to minimize the impact. The car bounced over the curb onto the sidewalk. Michael's door caught the back corner of one of the cop cars.

The passenger side slammed into a building as the little car spun. Michael fought the wheel left then right then back left. Katrina's head hit the roof as the car tumbled.

Chapter 5

The light was blinding. Strange beeping sounds. Heart monitor. Was she in the hospital? Her mind had very little to go on. Things were slow to come into focus. She tried to rub her eyes, but couldn't move her arms. Something pinning them. Handcuffs? That would make sense. She remembered two police officers coming to her door last night. Everything else seemed lost in a heavy fog.

Muffled voices echoed from the hall. She looked toward the sound and saw a large paneled oak door. This wasn't like any hospital she'd ever seen. The voices seemed to float out of the fog in her mind.

"I can't keep doing this. If the police found out, my license would be the least of my problems. I don't think you understand how serious this is. I mean, harboring and treating a fugitive? Really?"

"Doctor. You are being paid very well for your aid and silence in this matter. Beyond that, don't forget who actually pays for all that wonderful equipment at your newly remodeled hospital, not to mention your insane salary."

"Insane? How dare you? I earn every penny of that money doing stupid things like this for your *society*. I have to go. I'll be back to check on your *patient* tomorrow." Footsteps faded away on a stone floor. The door opened just a crack. Katrina saw an older man in a cardigan, plaid shirt and black pants slip through.

"Ahh. I see you're awake, Ms. Liu. Would it be alright if I called you Katrina?" She nodded. "My name is Father Daniel. I'm the head priest here at Our Lady of Victory Catholic Church."

"The Basilica?"

"You know it? Good. Your friend Thomas said you were in trouble, so I sent Michael to collect you. I hear you had an adventure. I guess we don't need these anymore." He pulled a key from his pocket and unlocked the handcuffs from her wrists. "A precautionary measure in case you woke up and started wandering around the church. I thought it was better if as few people as possible knew you were here."

"Michael?" Katrina tried to sit up, but the old man put a gentle hand on her shoulder.

"A remarkable young man, isn't he? More even than he's willing to admit, I'd guess. He's perfectly fine. He left to return to his studies with an old friend of mine down south. Probably a good idea since there's quite a bit of scuttlebutt around you two right now."

"Michael wasn't hurt in the crash?"

"Not a bit. As I said, he is quite a remarkable young man."

"Wait. Tommy? Who's Tommy?"

"Ahh, yes. You know him as Jim White. His real name is Thomas McKinney."

"I don't understand."

"Your friend is also a very unusual man, far more unusual than even Michael, judging from the evidence... but we will discuss all that later. Now you need to rest, doctor's orders." The elderly priest pushed a button on one of the machines attached to her. Katrina tried to protest, but her eyes closed on their own.

Chapter 6

There was a copper glow to her hair in the setting sun. Beautiful. He never got tired of it. She walked toward him across the field, making her way through the furrows. Ever graceful. Seamus trundled along behind, trying desperately to keep up.

He was glad to see her. He was always glad to see her, but right now especially. It had been a long and hot day. The pitcher in her hand was fresh, cool water. He took a huge drink and dumped the rest over his face before taking her in his arms and kissing her, long and passionately. She playfully tried to push him off, mumbling something about her dress and the mud and little Seamus. Then she giggled. That little girl giggle that made him well up. She was so soft in his arms, so vulnerable.

In six months it would be two years since they wed, in that tiny little chapel in the village. Her parents were unsure of a poor peasant farmer marrying their only child, but he had won them over. He was young, just nineteen. And poor, quite poor. But he worked hard and worked smart, and he convinced them that one day he could really make something of himself. They believed him. He watched her walk back to the tiny peat and sod hut they had made into a home. That beautiful frame silhouetted in the last rays of the setting sun.

A knock on the door later that night disturbed the peace of their evening. The voice behind it was even more disturbing. The landlord's man. Rent was due yesterday. Thomas knew it, but he had just gotten the coin together today. There was the usual unpleasantness and threats that he had come to expect since he agreed to farm this land, but they never came to anything. He worked his plot well, always brought in his crop, never filched or asked for support. He knew one day he would own this land, maybe open a shop in Dublin, selling hats or some such thing, somewhere far from the countryside of Cork, but for now, until he made his way, he was stuck working for the bloody English like everyone else in Ireland.

The next day was rain, but that didn't stop the work. He finished tilling and started planting the potatoes. He smoked his pipe in his favorite chair. Mary had just finished the washing up when there was another knock at the door. Thomas got up to answer while she saw to Seamus, who was fussing in his crib.

Thomas opened the door. Red coated British soldiers stood all around, ten of them with an officer, and the landlord's man. They were all armed but the landlord's man.

"Thomas McKinney?"

"'Tis me, yes."

"You were told by Mr. O'Riordan here that you were to vacate this land by this morning. We're here to remove you." The British officer didn't even look him in the eye when he spoke. Thomas felt his soul drop at the words.

"I was told no such thing. I paid him the rent yesterday. Paid in full, in silver."

"Now, that's an outright lie, McKinney. You told me yesterday that you didn't know when you would have the rent, and I'd have to move you by force. So here I am to do just that."

"By God, O'Riordan, you're a lying son of a bitch."

The landlord's man pushed past him into the home.

"Now, where is that lovely wife of yours?"

"Get out of my house, O'Riordan, or I swear I'll have ya." Thomas turned to grab the man, but a musket butt in the back dropped him to the floor.

"See what I was sayin', Captain? Undesirable temperament for a farmer. And by the way, it's my house now." He picked up little Seamus from the crib, giving him a good look over. "Lovely Mary can stay, of course." Thomas looked at his wife. She was standing by the fire. Fear and hatred filled her eyes. "This little bastard son of yours, well, I think he'll do fine in the workhouse." Thomas saw red. For the first time in his short life, he was angry beyond reason. He lunged from the floor for O'Riordan. He didn't make it. The British soldiers beat him down with their rifle butts before he could get his feet under him. He heard Mary scream. Through the blood in his eyes, he saw her make the lunge he couldn't. O'Riordan was the faster, and knocked her soundly on the head. She fell to the floor unconscious.

The soldiers lifted him to his feet and threw him out the door. He heard a wet thud next to him as Mary was tossed in the mud beside him. Thomas couldn't see Seamus, but he could hear that he was near his mother, crying hysterically.

There was another sound over the rain and the crying of his son. He focused on it as he lay there, covered in mud and blood. Laughing. O'Riordan and the British soldiers. Laughing at him and the horrible injustice they were doing. Thomas tried to stand, to fight for himself, but the beating recommenced. They were trying to pound him into the mud, to bury him alive on what was rightfully his own land. Even the Captain took his shots, probably for the inconvenience of having to come out in the rain. They shouted at him. They pulled him out of the mud and held his arms behind his back. That's when he saw the cart.

"Oh, that?" O'Riordan followed his gaze. "Well, since you can't pay your debts, and putting you in jail won't get me my money, Mary and little Seamus will be going to work to pay them off, that is, until you can pay off the sixty pounds sterling you owe for the past year's rent."

"I don't owe you any rent. I'm paid in full. I paid you yesterday."

"Captain, how long will it take for these two to work off sixty pounds debt in the workhouse?"

"About thirty years, if my math is right."

"Well, McKinney, looks like you'll either pay the money, or they'll both die in the workhouse." O'Riordan grinned and nodded at the soldiers as they grabbed Mary and Seamus. Two of them held Thomas back as Mary was loaded screaming into the barred cart with Seamus in her arms.

"Don't worry, Mary, I'll get you out. Whatever I have to do, I swear I'll free you. Just hold on.

The news came to him through the church in Dublin two years later. They were dead. Mary and Seamus. Cholera took them both in the workhouse. For the second time in his life, Thomas McKinney saw red. It was a deeper red now, a more permanent shade. Thomas did what he had done so many times in the intervening years. He dropped to his knees and prayed. He didn't pray for their safety, or that he would find the money to free them as had become his habit. He prayed for the will to extract the revenge he had earned. Tears splattered on the stones of the altar. He watched them fall, imagining each one a drop of blood from a British soldier's heart. He smiled. For the first time in two years he actually smiled. Watching that pool of blood form from his tears brought him a joy like nothing else he had known since the night they ripped his heart out. His smile turned into a chuckle, then a laugh. A deep heartfelt laugh that finally drowned out the screams of his wife and child. Screams he had heard non-stop for two years.

Hours later, he sat in a pub having a quiet drink with a man the locals only knew as *Riley*. Riley was a Fenian, or so they said. He spoke with a strange note in his voice. Rumors were he had spent several years in America after the Land War, but nobody really knew, since he never talked about himself or his past. If nothing else, he had no problem letting everyone know his feelings about the bloody British.

"Ya know, Tommy, there's a lot of peril in what you're thinking." Thomas looked up from his beer. He hadn't told anyone about his thoughts of revenge, or how he was considering acting on them. "That look in your eye, boyo. I know that look. Spent half my life seeing it in the mirror. But there's something you don't realize that could change your plans."

"What might that be, Riley?"

"That bastard landlord Williams and his little henchman aren't really the enemy. Just cogs in the wheel, my boy. Cut their heads off, two more grow back just like 'em."

"Then what do you think I should do? I can't let this lie, Riley. You know I can't."

"I don't expect you to, Tommy. But you have to understand your enemy before you strike out and miss your real target. You do that, and even if they let you live, you'll never have another chance. Prison here or Australia. Know who your real enemy is, boyo."

Tommy sat back in his chair.

"And who might that be, Riley?"

Riley leaned in. "The Famine Queen, Tommy."

Thomas' eyes widened. "There's no chance, Riley. I'd never get close. Do you really think I could get close?"

"Sonny, she's coming here. Wants to look in on her bastard Irish children. Big parade, the whole deal. I bet a man could get off, oh, five or even six shots before the guards could get to him in the crowd."

"You honestly think so?"

"I'd bet your life on it." Riley smiled.

Five months later. Tommy felt the weight of the pistol in his waistband. It was an American gun. A big Colt. He wished he had practiced with it. He had never fired a pistol, and now it felt too heavy pulling down on his belt. He kept his coat buttoned. There were guards everywhere. He tried not to look nervous. Did he look nervous? Could they see the bulge under his coat? So many bloody guards. He was on the curb, right at the edge of the barricade. Clear line of sight. Sweat beaded on his forehead, but it was a warm day, everyone out in their Sunday best to greet the Queen. Everyone was sweating.

Tommy smiled. His chance was coming. He didn't care if he lived or died. They were already dead. He wouldn't go to heaven for this, or maybe he would. The bitch was Protestant, anyway. Did Jesus care if you killed Protestants? He didn't know. Honestly, he didn't really care. He saw those tears making a pool of blood in the church, heard the screams of his wife and child as they were forced into the workhouse to labor as slaves, imagined their horrible deaths. Doing this wouldn't bring them back, but it might ease his heart to know Victoria would be in Hell with him. He wanted it. He wanted her blood on his hands.

His vision started to go red again. He fought it back as best he could. Had to shoot straight. Only got one shot at this. He could hear horses in the distance, just a couple of blocks away. Some in the crowd were cheering. He wished he could kill them too. There was no time for all that just now, maybe later on, but now he was focused. The first red coated guardsmen came around the corner. Their large plumed helmets seemed miles over his head. The Irish Guard. O'Riordan was one of them now, having traded in his rent collecting job for a commission in the Queen's army. He fought the urge to start shooting now. Looking up the street he saw the carriage trundling over the rough cobblestones toward him. Tears began to well up in his eyes as he thought of his beautiful Mary smiling, her red hair glowing in the sunset as Seamus dug in the dirt at her feet.

He wiped his eyes. He had to keep his vision clear. They were coming up the street now. In a moment the Queen would be just feet away, waving and looking down on her unwilling subjects. The first carriage guards passed by. Now the driver. He pulled the six shooter from his belt and aimed at the window of the carriage.

His eyes met hers. His were mad, glazed. Hers resolute, unwavering, stoic. He pulled the trigger six times. Six shots rang out and she didn't even move. Just sat staring at this madman who had just missed with six bullets from five feet away.

The guardsman hit him hard. By the time Thomas McKinney woke up, it was the next day, and he sat in the nastiest pit of a prison cell he could have ever imagined. He missed. He actually missed. His only chance. The screaming in his ears came back, louder than before. He screamed now, too. Frustrated, anguished screams, but the pain in his heart couldn't be exorcised by screaming or tears. Once again their faces haunted him. Gaunt, drawn faces now, dead from that horrible place.

Chapter 7

Waking from that particular nightmare was always harder than any other. He had fallen asleep in the library, that picture of Grozny and Rasputin and all their twisted allies was still in his hand. It was a solid reminder of what danger was really on the horizon. It was bigger than just somebody trying to elbow in on the local organized crime families, bigger than a murder. It was a fight for the city itself.

He had to find the man in that picture. Grozny was smart, though. He wouldn't leave much of a trail to follow. He'd had too many years practice avoiding the law. Hell, he had avoided the Russian Revolution. He had to find a link, someone to lead him to Grozny.

Tommy reached into his pocket and felt something small and metallic. He pulled it out and examined it: The big bastard's tie tack. In all the excitement of the past few days he had almost forgotten about it. It was nice, finely made, and gold. If they were based here, they wouldn't want to leave a trail by mail ordering these. They had to be made locally. Any artist who made things this nice would sign his work, and would remember who bought it. Tommy knew just the guy to ask. He rose and cleaned himself up.

Looking in the mirror, he realized something was off. Normally his fine vintage suits made him look more like an upper class businessman than a detective, but now they would make him stand out. He was laying low. He should dress to blend. Tommy went to the closet and pulled out a stuffed vacuum bag. Opening it, he pulled out a pair of jeans and a dark blue t-shirt. He slipped on the black Converse All-Stars he reserved for house work. There was an old black Carhartt jacket that he wore when he shoveled the sidewalk when he was staying here. He slipped on his shoulder holsters and the jacket over them. The jacket was bulky enough to hide his guns. He snapped just the bottom snap on the jacket to keep it from blowing open in the breeze.

Tommy walked a few blocks to a small house. It looked abandoned. Tommy didn't own this place, there was an old lady who lived here, but he rented her garage for *storage*. He turned the key in the lock and slid open the door. Pulling the tarp back, he saw the gleaming silver. She was just the way he had left her. He came by every few months to check on her, but there was little chance anything would happen. The old lady never left the house, and she was so paranoid that she would call the cops if a cat knocked over her trash can.

He pulled the key out of his pocket and started the engine. He had it worked on a few times, spent a ton of money upgrading everything from the brakes to the carburetor. It was a little light on power when it was new, but now it roared to life. He backed out of the garage and onto to the street.

There was nothing like the sound of that flat six Jaguar engine. Tommy loved it, always had. He babied this car. He didn't care if it was strange. There weren't many E-Types left, and this one was his. He had even gotten the rare detachable hard top. He could remember the day he walked into the dealership to buy it, this shiny silver machine. Over the years he had done everything he could to keep it running. Finding replacement parts was getting harder and harder, but he wouldn't give it up. It roared through the city even when he was just doing the speed limit. It stood out too much for detective work, he knew that. However, some things are just too good to give up.

Tommy pulled into the parking lot of the Basilica. Getting out of the car, he looked up at the gold spires, those symbols of hope and faith and sanctuary. He just prayed that Katrina had found sanctuary there, safety in the secrecy of the Catholic Church.

Walking into the huge entrance way, the cavernous space impressed him. It always had, ever since that first day so long ago when he had carried an injured old priest through these very doors.

Church had changed since he was younger. There was a time when at any point during the day if you walked into a major church like this, people would be milling about, praying to the various saints, talking quietly about church business, waiting to see a priest.

Now it was silent. Not even a cleaning crew between masses. Just the gurgling of the baptismal font and the sound of footsteps and the low conversation of church employees in the ante rooms behind the altar. Sometimes Tommy missed those days.

A plump old man walked toward him from one of the doorways on either side of the altar. There was an air about him, an ease and calmness. Tommy could tell he was a priest.

"Can I help you, my son?"

"Possibly, Father. I'm looking for someone who may have come to this church. Her name is Katrina Liu."

The Priest's demeanor shifted slightly. "I'm afraid I don't know that name, my son. Are you sure you have the right church?"

"Very sure, Father. I know she came here, and I know you're hiding her. I need you to bring her out to me."

"I don't know who you think you are, son, but you don't just walk into my church and demand to see someone. Especially someone who isn't here." The old priest was good. He held his ground.

"I'm Tommy McKinney."

"Are you really?"

"I am."

"And I'm supposed to believe you?"

"Father Baker sent me."

The priest's eyes widened. "My God. It is you. But, you haven't aged from Reverend Father's description. How is that possible?"

"It isn't, not by God's law. But I don't have time to explain, Father. Please take me to Katrina."

"Yes. Yes, of course. Please, follow me."

He led Tommy through a maze of passageways. Up and down flights of stairs, through doors and hallways, until even Tommy couldn't remember the path.

"Most people have no idea that there are so many different passages in our complex." The priest quipped. "Of course, Father Baker built this place as a sanctuary for souls, and there's no better refuge than the confusion of your pursuers."

Tommy couldn't agree more.

After ten minutes of walking, they came to a small door labeled "Rectory"

"This is the old entrance to the rectory. From the days when the priest didn't want to be seen before service, this let him slip into the church without running into nuns and employees, allowing him to collect his thoughts alone before mass."

"The good old days."

"That's what I've heard. But then, you'd know more about that than I would, wouldn't you?" The old priest had a twinkle in his eye.

They found Katrina in a small room that used to be reserved for the nuns who served the priest directly, his aids and secretaries. There was a time when they had to be on call twenty-four hours a day in case of emergency, and two or three of them at a time were allowed to stay in the rectory in this room. It looked like it hadn't been used in decades.

The door was open, but the priest knocked anyway. "Katrina, Thomas is here."

Katrina looked up from her book. "Nice to see you're okay, Mr. White. Or should I call you *Thomas McKinney*?"

"Tommy is fine. We have to go. I can't have the people who are after you coming into the church looking for you. Plus, I have a safer place. Get your things together, and I'll meet you in the sanctuary." Tommy turned the priest around and led him back down the hallway. "Father, would it be alright if I went back to the church and prayed for a while until Dr. Liu is ready?"

"Of course, my son. If you'd like, I'll take your confession."

"Thank you, but God is already punishing me for me sins."

"You know, Thomas, confessing our sins, especially ones of the nature of yours, can be a first step on the long road back to a holy life. Any normal person who has done what I believe you have would welcome the chance to atone. But there's nothing normal about you, is there?"

"Father, normal is something I gave up on years ago."

"I suppose it is."

She gathered her things quickly. There wasn't much, just a few articles of clothing she had managed to grab before being rushed out of her house, and her iPhone. She never went anywhere without her iPhone. It all fit in the small duffle bag Father Daniel had given her a few days ago when she was first able to get up and move around. Her injuries from the crash hadn't been too terrible. A couple of broken ribs that were healing well and a concussion. She often thought of the young man who had rescued her. Michael. What had become of Michael? She was knocked out when he crashed the car into the road block, but how did they get away? From the fierceness he had shown in her apartment, he might have taken on all of those cops. Could he have, really? And how could he drive like that? He seemed to know where every turn was; he ran red lights like he had known when there would be cars coming and when there wouldn't: Slowing for some, flying through others.

As she made her way through the winding hallways to the church, Katrina heard low conversation coming from the altar. She made her way to the back of the church so as to not interrupt. A single figure kneeled before the crucifix.

"He is an uncommon man. My dear, there is something I think you need to see." Father

Daniel had walked up behind her in that stealthy way that older people had of moving without being noticed. He put his arm around her waist and led her from the nave. They left Tommy praying quietly in Latin.

The shades were drawn in Father Daniel's office. They had been ever since the night she woke up in the basement operating room. She took a seat opposite his desk as he rummaged through a drawer in the ancient slab of oak. He made a small exclamation, apparently finding what he was looking for.

"Here it is." An old envelope. Very old. "This has been passed down from one Monsignor to the next since Father Baker. He was the man who built the cathedral you see today." He showed her the letter.

"Is this Latin?" She handed it back.

"Yes, Latin. But also in mirror writing. It was a trick DaVinci used to protect his notes. Father Baker was a great lover of the old master. This is the only time we know of that he used DaVinci's cypher to encode a message. For that matter, this is the only encoded message we know of that he ever wrote."

"It must be something important."

"Like I said, it has been passed down from Monsignor to Monsignor. No one else has ever been told about it, much less what it contains."

"So, what does it say?"

"It talks of an Irishman who saved Father Baker from a group of thugs one night. Here, let me quote him:

'He will come back to this church one day; I have given him leave to ask for sanctuary here. An unusual man, a dark and pained man, with a soul covered in shadow. He has called himself by many names, but he won't lie about his name in this church. It is Thomas McKinney.'"

Katrina stared blankly at the wall. The old priest continued:

"We've always wondered if Father Baker had started to lose his faculties in his old age, but it seems he was quite right when he wrote this."

"I don't understand. Did he predict that this would happen, that I'd be here? Was it some kind of holy premonition?"

"My dear, he describes our friend Thomas as the man who saved him. I don't think you're getting the point. This letter is dated 3 July, 1933."

"There's no way he's that old. He's not a day over 27."

"He owns that building his office is in, and those pistols he carries are vintage, much older than me. I knew an officer in World War Two who carried the same guns."

"I don't believe it. It's not possible."

"Well, believe it or not, my dear. But our Thomas, the man you met as Jim White, is a hundred years old, if not older." Katrina walked out of the office, her head swimming.

Tommy met her in the church. He walked her out to the car and they drove the few miles to his safe house in silence. He pulled the small sports car into the abandoned looking garage and closed the door.

After getting Katrina settled, he went up to his library to consider the case. But it was more than a case now, wasn't it? Now it was what he had been looking for most of his life. He took his guns out and set them on a small table by the door. Pulling several volumes off the shelf, he stood at the research desk and studied them in detail. He didn't even hear her come in.

"What are you looking at?" Katrina was standing in the doorway.

"Books, old books and manuscripts. Trying to figure out how this all went down. Right now it doesn't make much sense."

"Tell me about it. A month ago I was making great progress on a huge scientific discovery, now I'm a fugitive and a murder suspect. I was going to win the Noble Prize for what I discovered."

"You didn't discover it."

"I'm sorry, what?"

"You didn't discover it. Come here, look." Tommy led her over to the table. "You see this drawing here?" He pointed to a hand drawn image of what looked like a complex mechanical calendar.

"Yes."

"This is a drawing of the Antikythera Device. It was found around nineteen hundred off the coast of the Greek island of the same name. It's made of brass, and was designed by Archimedes. This drawing was made in seventeen eighty one."

"But how is that possible if it wasn't found until nineteen hundred?"

"It wouldn't be, but it was never really lost."

"What do you mean?"

"Well, this one was lost, but the technology to make them, and other devices like them was never lost. It was held by a small group of men throughout the ages, closely guarded."

"But what's so special about a calendar?"

"It's not a calendar. Well, they don't think it was. This is the only surviving one. The scholars who studied it thought it might have been a time travel device."

"A time machine? Archimedes invented a *time machine*?"

"Well, yes. For the king of Syracuse. You see, you didn't discover dark energy, he did. And he mastered it. He found a way to use a special alloy of brass to harness and control the energy. That sample that was sent to your lab? That was it."

"So if what you're saying is true, this alloy must directly transfer from radiation to kinetic energy. That's a huge advance. This could change the world. I mean, it could potentially solve all our energy problems."

"It does more than just that. It can be manipulated to do almost anything, even stop time."

"Stop time?"

Tommy looked into her. She could feel his eyes pressing into the back of her skull.

"Father Daniel showed you the letter?"

"He did, yes." She looked at the floor.

"Then you know that I'm not just a detective. The truth is; I'm one hundred and forty two years old this year."

"How is that possible?"

"I was born in Ireland in eighteen seventy. The landlord's man stole my land, forced my wife and baby boy into slavery in the workhouse to pay a debt I didn't owe. I tried to get my revenge by killing the queen."

"Queen Victoria?"

"That's the one. I was transported to Australia for my crime with another man, I only knew him as Riley. Anyway, while there, I noticed that one of the British officers seemed to be able to be everywhere at once. He was always where you didn't want him to be. I saw that before he caught whoever was breaking the rules, he played with this pocket watch he carried. I got it in my head that it was the watch that was letting him move so quickly."

"It was a device."

I didn't know it at the time, but yes, it was. Of course with everything that had happened, by that time I was a steadfast Fenian, and figured that the watch could help us escape and maybe help free Ireland from British rule."

"So you stole it?"

"In a way. This old officer had a habit of taking a walk around the camp in the evenings. One night Riley and I snuck out after dinner and waited for him. We hid at the corner of a storage shed, and when he passed, I wrapped a rope around his neck."

"You killed him?"

"Yes, he was the first. He certainly wasn't the last. Using the watch, we escaped the camp and stole some civilian clothes and money. We got to Sydney and on a boat to the U.S. Riley had lived there for a few years and had friends that could get us work while we waited for things to cool down at home.

When we got to the States, Riley and I went our separate ways. He headed west, figuring he'd live out his days in San Francisco or somewhere like that. I stayed in the East. I hadn't told Riley, but there was an engraving on the inside of the watch, the name of the maker. It said: 'A. Merrick & Co. Buff. NY'"

"That's how you came to Buffalo?"

"Round about. I had no money, and to avoid detection, we had entered through the port of New Orleans. It took me years to get to Buffalo. I got here the first time in 1898. I had found A. Merrick & Co. The owner was Adalai Merrick. He was a watchmaker. I didn't know it at the time, but watch-making was one of the key crafts for making a device. The other was metallurgy."

"The brass gear."

"Exactly. But by the time I got here, Merrick had disappeared. His granddaughter, who was barely eighteen, was running the shop, and she was being followed by some Russians. I figured they were after the same information I was, and they didn't look as sweet and cuddly as me. So I made plans without her knowledge to get her out of the city."

"What happened?"

"I came to get her one night, and three Russians were right behind me. They chased us through South Buffalo to the canal, where my boat was supposed to be waiting. We got there before the boat and the Russians had us cornered." I tried to activate the watch before the bullets started flying, but one of their rounds went through it while it was in my hand." Tommy held up his left hand and revealed a ragged circular scar in the middle of his palm. "I pushed the girl into the water before they shot me four more times, knocking me into the canal as well."

Katrina's mouth was slightly open, her eyes wide. "Then what?"

"Well, I couldn't move. I was floating on the canal. I could hear the girl crying for a couple minutes, then everything went silent. By the time the boat got there, the girl and the Russians were gone. I figured the girl drowned and the Russians left us both for dead."

"The watch. It was active when the bullet destroyed it?"

"Yes. It took me about four years to figure out that I wasn't aging. I got hurt. Got hurt a lot, and even came close to death a few times, but I never died, and every time, my body seemed to return to the way it was right before the watch was destroyed. I got scars, but no permanent damage. It wasn't more than a few days ago that I was shot through the side and dislocated my kneecap." Tommy untucked his shirt and showed Katrina fresh, pink scars on the front and back of his right side. "Not a single grey hair. Nothing. Never even caught a cold. The best I could figure is whatever energy these things work on, some of it must have been in the shards of brass that went into my body when that watch exploded in my hand, freezing me at that moment. I spent the next fifty years trying to find a way to remove this curse."

"That's very possible. If the radiation stays with the metal, then it could take hundreds of years for it to decay, if ever. Is it really a curse, though?"

"I can't die, Katrina. Everyone I know grows old and dies; goes to heaven or hell. I'm trapped here, forever."

"But if you don't want it, why don't you end it yourself?"

Tommy's eyes narrowed. "Suicide is a mortal sin. I do that; I'll never see heaven, never see Mary and Seamus again. My only choice is to try to atone for my sins, for the men I've killed, for the lives I've destroyed. And maybe then, God will show me the way to the watchmaker, the man who might be able to remove this stain."

"But you've killed men since. You've killed men recently. Isn't that a sin?"

"These men I've killed, they were under the influence of the devices. When a man gets like that, he is no longer a man. He is a monster. The radiation affects them, effects their minds. If I did kill men, it was mercy for me to do so."

"Has it affected your mind, too?"

"There are some people, a few, who are immune to it, like a disease immunity. Most who are exposed for any period of time suffer from dementia, schizophrenia, paranoia. It's incurable."

"So the ones who are immune, they're the ones who become watchmakers?"

"A few do, maybe two or three in any generation. Many years ago, around the time of the story I just told you, a Russian monk started a cult based around devices. He drew powerful people to him, made them think he was a prophet, a seer. He used the fact that the devices drove people mad to his advantage, turning them insane and then controlling them. He even enslaved a watchmaker and forced him to make devices for his cult. He was planning to take over the world." Tommy pointed to a picture on his desk. "That's the guy who's trying to kill you. He is a follower of that cult. He and his brother and his master were the three Russians on the canal that night." Tommy got up and pushed in his chair.

"These devices, how many are there?"

"I don't know. All my research is here. Manuscripts covering over two millennia. A lot of them are listed, the makers were experimenters, and many of them were early scientists, so they tracked their progress. But the darker ones made no notes about what they were doing, and there's no way to know how many of the records were lost, or burned during the Inquisition, or destroyed before they could fall into the wrong hands. I know for a fact that the Nazis were hunting for devices all over the world."

"You said that these records go back two thousand years?"

"More than. Some are copies of earlier documents, some are translations. Here, look at this." Tommy went over to a cabinet and pulled on a pair of white cotton gloves. He reached into a pigeonhole and pulled out a scroll. It was heavily yellowed, apparently ancient. He went over to a long table and rolled out part of it. "This is Greek. Saved with a few other of the same type from the burning of the library in Alexandria by Julius Caesar, as far as we know. The others I have not been able to find yet."

"This is from the library of Alexandria? I thought everything in the library was burned with it."

"That was kind of the point. Caesar didn't want anyone to have this knowledge. That's why he burned the library in the first place. Who knows what secrets were actually lost in that fire? Do you read Greek?"

"No, they didn't cover ancient Greek in my physics doctoral program."

"Shame, they should've. I made a translation. It's on that table. You'd probably do well to familiarize yourself with it; I'm going to need your help."

"With what?"

"I understand the Greek, what I don't understand is the science."

Tommy headed toward the door.

"Where are you going?"

"I have to find out how he survived."

"Who? That guy in the picture?"

Tommy slid the pistols into holsters under his arms.

"Listen. Whatever he's calling himself now; his real name is Vladimir Grozny. If he's come back to Buffalo, Hell isn't very far behind."

"You think one man is behind all this?"

"If he's here, then he's suffered the same effects I have, or he found another way to keep from dying. After recent events, it looks like he's trying to continue his master's work."

"But who was his master?"

"Grigori Rasputin." Tommy put on his coat and walked out of the room.

Katrina looked down at the picture. There was Grozny, shaded granny glasses resting low on his nose. The man next to him was a face familiar to anyone who'd taken a European History class. Holy shit, it really was Rasputin.

Chapter 8

The paranoia that had served Tommy so well for so long was going haywire. As he stood on the sidewalk every noise, every passing car, every voice in the distance was a threat. Every drop of condensation from a window air conditioner high above was the nearby footstep of an enemy.

He watched the windows of the pawn shop across the street. Dave Pinsky's place. Dave wasn't a bad guy, per se, but he was one of the best, and therefore most popular, fences in the city. Everybody had to make money.

Tommy knew that Dave would be able to tell him where Big 'Un was. That was the first link. Step one on the ladder to finding out what Grozny was up to. He couldn't go straight to Grozny. He knew better. Grozny wouldn't talk. He was a fanatic. Tommy figured that without his master, he couldn't muster that fanaticism in others.

He stepped across the street and into the dank little pawn shop. Dave was nowhere to be seen, but Tommy knew he was there. The greasy little man smoked acrid Indian cigarettes that stank of clove. The smell fouled the air in the tiny shop.

"Pinsky. I know you're here. Get out here." Tommy waited. "Pinsky! I want to talk to you." There was a noise in the back of the shop. The little fence stepped through a door behind the counter.

"Jesus Christ. Jim White. You're supposed to be dead. I can't be talking to you. You're hot, man, real hot."

"Come on, Dave. You've handled hotter. And I left you alone about it, didn't I? As far as you know, I am dead."

"Yeah, I got ya, Jim. I got ya. Come around back, away from the windows." Jim followed him to a small alcove behind rows of shelves.

"What does the dead man want from me?"

Tommy pulled a tie pin from his pocket.

"Recognize this? Took it off a bruiser who jumped me a few days ago. Big guy, real big. You know who made it?" Pinsky put his hands up.

"I can't talk about that. I don't know nothin' about that." Tommy grabbed the little man by the collar and pressed a pistol against his forehead.

"I'm not fucking around with you, Dave. Your life depends on the next thing you say."

"Okay, okay." Tommy lowered the gun. "I don't know the name of the jeweler. But the guy you described, yeah, I know that son of a bitch. Name's Ted Barnes. Don't get caught up in that, Jim. It's serious bad news. He's got major connections."

"How so?"

"Well, I don't know much, and what I do know, I don't know, understand?" Tommy nodded. "Seems that ol' Teddy and a few other guys can get away with pretty much anything now. They've got connections, way up."

"Where can I find him?"

"He's usually at Kelly's on the south side. That's where he does most of his business." Tommy got up and started walking out. You're not seriously going after him, White. They'll kill you. Simple as that."

"Good thing I'm already dead." Tommy deadpanned.

Kelly's was a dive. Had been for fifty years. Tommy walked through the door into a cloud of smoke. They banned smoking in public places in Buffalo years ago, but places like this weren't really public. Locals only, and if they don't know you, they don't like you. Tommy didn't want service. He wanted Big 'Un.

Even through the gloom he could tell he was being watched. He sat at a table near the door and scanned the room. A rode-hard waitress brought him a coaster and he ordered a beer, dropping four bucks on her tray. He felt her disgust at the poor tip and scanned the room. Groups of men sat huddled together. There was more than one crime being planned here.

There was Barnes. Sitting in the corner furthest from the door against a wall. That huge frame in a fitted suit hulking in a chair that looked like it was about to give up the ghost. There were four other men at the table. He couldn't make out their faces clearly, but none of them looked like saints. He couldn't confront Barnes with all that backup. The waitress sloshed his beer down on the table and walked away.

Barnes got up and walked to the front door. As he passed Tommy he seemed somehow different. The thug bravado was gone. There was a quiet confidence now, a self-assuredness in his stride. Something had seriously changed him in the past few days.

Tommy waited a couple of minutes for him to get away from the door then followed. The group of men had walked around behind the bar to several dark sedans in the alleyway. There was no way he was getting to the big man without going through the rest of them.

Dead end alley, two cars. Tommy watched from around the corner on the sidewalk. The men got into different cars. Barnes got into the second one, backseat behind the driver. The other three men got into the first. They started to pull out of the alley. The first car made a left past Tommy. The second made a right. Barnes was alone in the backseat.

Tommy saw his chance. As the car began to accelerate, he caught up and wrenched open the back door. Jumping into the moving car, he pulled a pistol and jammed the barrel under Big 'Un's chin. The driver looked back, and Tommy motioned him to keep driving.

"White. They said you were probably dead. I didn't figure I'd see you again."

"Yeah, I just keep running into you in the strangest places."

"What do you want, White?"

"I want to know where I can find your boss."

"Tony, stop the car." The driver pulled up to the curb. The big man turned to Tommy. "Listen White. You don't get it. We're untouchable. Now that I know you're still around, even if you make it out of this car alive, we'll chase you down. We run this city."

"Oh, really?" Tommy cocked the revolver.

"You think I'm afraid of death? I've found a new faith, White. The one *true* faith. Dying for my faith will only bring me closer to God." Tommy pulled out his other pistol and pressed it against the back of the driver's head.

"Does Tony feel the same way?" The driver didn't flinch. Barnes laughed.

"You see? You're in over your head, White. There's nothing you can do that will make any of us give up our Order."

"Your order, huh? What order would that be?"

Barnes smiled. "Yeah, not telling you that, neither."

"Where's Grozny? Where does your boss stay?"

"You wanna talk to the boss? You really do have a death wish, don't you?"

"I guess I must. So where is he?"

"I'm not telling you, White."

"I'll tell you what I'm going to do. I've got twelve bullets. I'm going to start at your feet. One bullet each. Then your ankles, then your knees. What's that make? Six. Right. Then I'll shoot you in the balls. If you're still with me, I'll keep working my way through the painful spots."

"Even you're not crazy enough to try that here. I got people waiting for me. They'll start looking if I don't show up. You don't have enough bullets for *that*."

Tommy moved the gun he had trained on Tony's head and shot Barnes in the left foot. Barnes screamed.

"I'm still not telling you. What they'll do to me is way worse than anything you could imagine."

Tommy shot his other foot. Tony still hadn't even flinched.

"I told you, I can't say anything. They'll kill me."

"So will I. You still doubt that?" Tommy shot him in the left knee. The big man screamed and started crying. "Maybe I should just jump to the main event?" Tommy pointed the gun at Barnes' balls.

"Ok, ok. I met him once, picked him up when I first joined the Order. He was staying at a flop house on the east side. Cleveland drive, out by the airport."

"I know the place."

"Good. If you're going to find him, that's the only place I know to look. I swear. Oh God, they're going to kill me, they're really going to kill me."

"I suppose there's only one thing to do, then." Tommy sighed

"You're going to protect me now, right?"

"Nope." Tommy pulled both triggers. Glass shattered as forty five caliber bullets passed through their targets and the windows of the car beyond. The car horn blared under the weight of the driver's ruined skull. He looked at Barnes' expressionless face.

"I was thinking, 'Send you to your God,' but whatever." He stepped out of the car and walked away.

Tommy ducked into an alley. His head was swimming. Images flashed from the past. A coldness engulfed him. He tried to shake it off. He fell through a foggy night, his body riddled with holes. Electricity burned his nerves. Echoes of gunshots filled the air. Somewhere in the distance, a carriage rattled along cobblestone streets. There, through the fog and gun smoke, he saw that face. The face from the picture. Vladimir Grozny. The scars on either side of his left hand burned. Shiny shards of shattered gears, glass, and brass floated in the space between them.

A car horn pulled him back. He was still in the alley, half a block from where he had just killed two men. His legs were shaky. Sirens echoed in the distance. He walked up a block and hailed a cab.

Back at the safe house, Tommy kneeled in prayer. He didn't hear Katrina come in behind him. She waited for him to finish and spoke up.

"Did you find him?"

"No."

"So, what's our next step?"

"My next step is to move up the ladder. I have to find Grozny. Your next step is to keep your head down and make plans to get as far from here as you can."

"I'm not going anywhere. This is as much my problem as yours. I want to help."

"These aren't the kind of people you can reason with, Katrina. They won't listen, just kill you or worse, make you an example. I can't allow that." Tommy looked in her eyes. He knew that look. She trusted him with her life. He had seen that look twice before, and failed them both.

"I've already talked to Father Daniel. He has connections; he'll get you out of the States and to a church in Switzerland. No extradition. You'll be safe from the law there. Until I deal with Grozny, you won't really be safe anywhere, but the church has experience hiding people, they'll do their best until it's over."

"I'm not leaving, Tommy. Look, I've been doing some research. The number of spikes in radiation increased dramatically just after the mayoral elections last year. Do you think it could have anything to do with this Grozny guy?"

"I don't think, I know. Rasputin bent a cult of heretics called the Khlysty to his will and started collecting devices to try and take over Russia. The student has picked up where the master left off. But something doesn't make sense."

"What's that?"

"Well, there aren't that many devices. The skills to make them are really rare. I mean, we're talking about maybe fifty or sixty in all of history. Most of them have been destroyed."

"So how many are we talking about now?"

"Maybe eight or nine left, max, and they're not that powerful. There's no way Grozny could get this much influence with just the ones left, even if he had all of them. Beyond that, why here? There are more influential places to start than Buffalo."

"Maybe he figured out how to make more?"

"That's impossible. He'd need..." Tommy's face went white.

"Need what?"

"A watchmaker who already had the knowledge. And a forge."

"A forge?"

Tommy pulled a bunch of rolled papers out of a drawer and spread them on the table. Old maps of the city.

"The alloy of brass is incredibly hard to reproduce. The ingredients are very specific. Get it wrong by even the slightest percentage and you get nothing but plain old metal. It would take a lot of time, and a place no one would notice someone forging metal."

"Buffalo's full of abandoned steel mills."

"That explains why he chose this city. It's also how we find him."

"But how do we know which one they're in? Between the steel mills and other abandoned factories in this city, he could be anywhere."

"We find an ant and follow it back to the hill."

Tommy put his jacket on and picked up one of his pistols.

"Why revolvers? Doesn't a modern pistol hold more bullets?"

"Anybody worth giving a gun to doesn't need more than six shots."

Katrina picked his second gun up off the table with two fingers.

"Sometimes twelve." He took the gun from her and checked the cylinder, sliding it into the shoulder holster.

Chapter 9

Tommy stood at the end of the hallway in the flickering fluorescents. What was that smell? Dog piss? No, worse. Human. He hated these places. As he walked down the hall, he could hear the noise from within the different first floor apartments. Here a crying baby, there a television blasting out the words of a fire-and-brimstone preacher who had no idea this particular member of his flock was shooting heroin as he shouted out the word of God.

He could smell that, too. The drugs. They had a particular stink that it took days to wash off. But that wasn't what brought him here. He stepped through the filth to the desk of this pay-by-month shit hole. The attendant's scent nearly choked him. Sausage link fingers held desperately to an ancient issue of *Massive Juggs* while grease dripped a complex pattern of stains onto a grey tank top that may have once been white.

"Where's Grozny?" Tommy asked. The man shifted his eyes to Tommy, then back to his porno. "OK, then. Politeness doesn't work. Let's try again." Tommy grabbed the man's shirt and pressed the barrel of his revolver against the greasy forehead. He'd have to remember to wash his gun later.

"Room two-twelve." The man grunted, seeming remarkably unimpressed at having a gun shoved in his face.

Tommy let him go and turned to walk away, then realized his mistake. Shifting his eyes back to the counter, he saw the man reaching for the telephone. He was calling one of two people: The cops or Grozny. Most likely Grozny, but neither would do. Tommy leapt across the counter and snatched the receiver from his hand.

"Sorry, lad. But I can't have you doing that." The man attempted to lift his enormous girth, but Tommy pulled out his gun and struck him in the side of the face. The man crumpled to the floor. Was he dead? Tommy wondered for a minute, then realized that he didn't really care. He holstered the pistol and walked to the stairs.

The second floor was no better than the first. If anything, the filth was thicker up here. What would drive a man like Vladimir Grozny to a place like this? The guy had more money than he knew what to do with. Of course, that was the problem. What he found to do with his money was the reason Tommy was looking for him. He studied things no one had the right to. He had answers. Tommy needed those answers.

Two-twelve. Tommy tried the knob. Locked, of course. Nothing was ever easy. Kick in the door? No, too noisy. Clubbing that beached whale desk clerk was more exposure than he wanted, busting in a door would just draw even more attention. He looked at the small circular scar in the palm of his left hand and the dark flecks within it. Just on the other side of this flimsy chunk of wood was one of the men that put it there. Tommy tasted metal.

Taking a step back, he put the full weight of his body against the door. It came easily off its hinges. Tommy drew both pistols and stepped into chaos.

Grozny turned and ran at Tommy, a huge black gauntlet on his right arm. Tommy managed to dodge the first swing, the gloved hand punching a large hole in the wall. The return swing glanced off of Tommy's shoulder, knocking him onto the floor in the hall. One of his pistols clattered against the wall.

Grozny's face looked possessed, his eyes wild with rage. He stood over Tommy lying amongst the detritus of sin. Tommy barely managed to shuffle out of the way before the black fist struck the floor, cracking the tile. Struggling to his feet, he turned to see that huge black fist way too close to his left eye.

His body cracked plaster as he hit the wall before sliding dazed to the floor. Grozny leaned over and lifted Tommy off the ground by the throat with his metal right hand.

"Do you know this device, Mr. McKinney?"

"Part of the Black Armor." Tommy coughed.

"Good. Then you know what it does?"

"Yes." Tommy managed a bloody grin. "It makes you stupid." He cocked the other revolver under Grozny's chin as he held the black gauntlet with his opposite hand.

"Hmm. I squeeze, you shoot. But the gauntlet continues to squeeze. It would seem that I have, shall we say, the upper hand?"

Tommy could feel consciousness slipping as he considered the Russian's horrible pun. He had to think of something. Upper hand...

Tommy turned the pistol on the armored wrist and fired. The blast knocked the gun from Tommy's hand. Shards of brass and blood and bone splattered his face. The crushing hand relaxed as Grozny shrieked. Both men fell to the floor.

Pulling the gauntlet off Grozny's ruined right hand, Tommy reached into his pocket and set his watch against it. Opening the case, he saw that the movement was completely stopped, no energy to run it. Just what he wanted.

Returning his attention to Grozny, he lifted the mangled hand. Again Grozny shrieked. Tommy pulled the signet ring off the finger it had called home for so long. He took a moment to examine the crest and Cyrillic writing on its face before holding it up in front of Grozny.

"Where are they made? Where is the brass works?"

Grozny looked away. Tommy squeezed his wrist tighter.

"Who's the watch maker? Who's building the devices?"

Once again, Grozny refused to answer. Tommy squeezed again, and Grozny howled in pain. Tommy shoved the ring in his mouth and pinned Grozny's mouth and nose shut until he swallowed. Picking up his pistol from the floor, Tommy showed it to Grozny.

"Do you remember this gun? You should. It's the one I took off you in front of Merrick's. Long time ago, wasn't it? Figured you'd be dead by now. Bet you wished the same of me." Tommy smiled and looked at the scar on Grozny's forehead. It was ragged, as though he had never gotten proper care for the wound.

"I have a message for your boss. You tell him that I'm still alive, and I'll find him, even if it takes forever. You tell him Tommy McKinney is still alive." Tommy pressed the barrel of the pistol against Grozny's knee and fired. Grozny passed out. Maybe from shock, more likely from losing the energy the gauntlet had given him.

Pulling himself to his feet, Tommy limped down the hall, picking up his other pistol. It the distance he could hear sirens.

"Ah, the great citizens of Buffalo." Tommy thought. "Gunfire and screaming, and they still wait ten minutes to call the cops."

Slipping out the door into the alley behind the building, Tommy disappeared into the city.

Chapter 10

The church was quite when Tommy returned. A few worshipers still lingered after the evening mass. Father Daniel was behind the sacristy locking up the communion. Tommy approached the altar, genuflected, and got the old priest's attention.

"Did you find what you were looking for, Thomas?"

"I sent the message I intended to send, if that's what you mean."

"Thomas, there's something I feel I need to discuss with you."

"What's that, Father?"

"You and I both know what kind of man you are, Thomas, what you've done. It's my duty to council you that there has to be a better way. You know what The Lord teaches about *murder*." He whispered these last words, nervously glancing around the church.

"I know full well what the Bible teaches. I also know that if this heresy is allowed to spread that a lot of innocent people will suffer."

"Thomas, think of your soul. There is no excuse for murder."

"I'm a damned man, Father. I will never see the Kingdom. Don't you see that? I can't die. I can't end my own life. I'm trapped here. Punishment for a lifetime of evil."

"Do you think committing more evil will make your situation *better*?"

"It can't make it worse. Did Katrina get away safely?"

"I don't know. She didn't come here. I figured she went straight to the airport. She did send a note though, through email. She said she found the foundry, whatever that means. Said it's the abandoned one on Vulcan Street. She left instructions that I should give you the note, she said you'd know what it meant.

The sun was just setting as Tommy reached the fence of the dilapidated factory.

The was no light visible in the buildings, but these guys were too smart to leave a clue like that. After checking for sentries, he climbed the fence and dropped into enemy territory. A faint smile twisted on his lips. This was just like the old days, but with bigger guns.

He was still smiling as he sprinted across the open space to the nearest building. Clouds filled the sky, letting only a dim light reflect off the railroad tracks that crisscrossed the yard like huge scars. In the shadow of a massive office building he scanned the buildings further into the yard, closer to the lake. The yellowed windows kept him from seeing inside most of them, others had no windows left at all, just gaping hollow eye sockets staring back at him out of weatherworn blackened brick faces.

Then there it was. A glimmer. A reflection. A shaft of light shining from a doorway. Tommy squinted at the sky over the building. Smoke. Just a wisp. They were using minimum capacity. Probably only working at night. Tommy bolted from shadow to shadow, moving ever closer in a zig zag. He knew they had guards. There had to be men outside the building, at least to keep the transients and drug addicts away.

Finally he was yards from the door. The dumpster he crouched behind was too new to have been left here when the factory closed. He watched the lit doorway, checking for movement, a break in the beam, anything to give away who might be there.

Chapter 11

Tommy saw a small door near an unlit corner of the building. He made his way to the wall and checked it: There was a large steel bar blocking it from being opened from the inside. He carefully lifted the bar out of place and looked around. No guards in sight. Tommy slipped through the door. There were strange sounds coming from the darkness. Even as his eyes adjusted, he could not discern the source of the noise. Gears grinding. A clanking on the concrete floor. The sound of a bellows.

"Get out, son." The voice was a raspy, soft whisper coming from the shadows. "You need to get out."

"I *need* to get to the factory floor."

"There's no getting out there, my boy. They have guards at the door and more beyond. If you try to get onto the floor, you'll be as trapped as I am."

"And who would you be?" The clanking came closer. Tommy saw a brass foot and ankle appear from the shadows. A horrid, distorted face looked down on him. One eye looked like a camera lens. There were no teeth in the gaping mouth.

"Adalai Merrick, at your service."

As the figure stepped into the light, Tommy got a better look at him. A large brass plate was riveted to the bare chest. On it was an amazingly intricate clockwork mechanism. Two hoses punched out of the right side of the chest and over the shoulder to an apparatus on the back.

"*The* Adalai Merrick? The watchmaker?"

"I was once. Now I am this." The man gestured with a mechanical hand at his own body.

"But, you disappeared. You disappeared in eighteen ninety-eight."

The man turned his face to the darkness.

"I had no choice. They were going to kill her. My granddaughter. My little Eliza."

"But, they did kill her. I was there."

"You? Impossible."

"I found your watch. I came to Buffalo to find you. You were already gone, but the Khlysty were after her. There was a gunfight. The watch was destroyed while I was using it. She fell in the canal, Mr. Merrick. There's no way she didn't drown."

Merrick spun around.

"She *didn't* drown." The raspy whisper turned into a growl. "I watched her grow up. I watched her grandchildren grow up as I became more and more of a monster. She did what I taught her. She changed her name, tried to hide her identity. She carried on."

"She didn't drown?"

"Of course not, you fool! If she was gone do you honestly think I would have kept working for these bastards? They followed her, followed her family like a dark shadow all these years. Threatening generation after generation of my family to keep me working." The mechanical fist clenched rhythmically. "You said that the watch broke while you were using it?"

"Yes."

"Was Grozny there? How close was he?"

"Within pistol range. His bullet broke the watch." Tommy rubbed his palm.

"The energy wave must have engulfed all of you. That explains why he's aged so little over the years. But, there's something different between the two of you."

Tommy held up his palm. "Some shards of brass went into me when the bullet went through my hand."

"Ahh. So that's what it is. The brass was energized when it got embedded in you. It's a part of your system now, just as these parts are a part of mine." Merrick tapped the plate on his chest with his human hand.

"So there's no way to reverse it?"

"None that I'm aware of. If the watch had survived, maybe I could have done something with it to try to reverse the process, but after so many years, reversing it would most likely make you die of old age."

"That would be a blessing. Do you know what they're doing here?"

"They're making me build a device. Not just any device, either. It is massive. There are blueprints that they keep locked up in the office upstairs. Some of the parts they already have, and they are ancient. Possibly original devices."

"What is it for?"

"I haven't a clue. I can tell that what I'm building is an amplifier, but what I'm amplifying, I don't know." The strange creature's head snapped toward the door. "They're coming for me. Go back the way you came, now!"

A deadbolt slid back just as Tommy slipped through the outside door, holding it closed tight.

"Come on, old man." One of the guards said. "Time to get back to work."

Tommy heard Merrick shamble into the foundry.

Tommy slipped through the door after them. He was just paces behind, but the darkness was only broken by the flashlights on their assault rifles, and they were too confident to think anyone would be stupid enough to try and sneak in behind them. After traveling through what seemed like miles of hallways, they finally arrived in a huge room lit by the glow of molten metal. It was an old school foundry, with a catch pit in the middle of the floor below the crucible. Over the pit was a shallow tray filled with molten tin. They were making sheets of brass by floating the metal out on the tin and letting it cool.

Tommy watched from behind a pillar as the two guards led Merrick around the catch pit to a man who was standing at the base of the stairs. Tommy couldn't see him clearly, but figured it had to be Vladimir Grozny's brother, Ivan. The two men exchanged words, and Merrick went to work adding chemicals to the crucible.

Then Tommy saw something he didn't expect: Two men came out of the office and started down the stairs. The first was in handcuffs. Then two more figures appeared in the doorway. The one in the rear leaned on a cane. The first one seemed smaller, possibly a woman.

As the four people reached the bottom of the stairs, their faces were illuminated by the glow of the liquid metal. Fuck. It was Kowalski leading Scotty, and behind them, Grozny led Katrina.

"Come on out, White. We know you're here." Kowalski sounded as arrogant and stupid as ever. "Unless you want your friends to die right here."

Tommy did a quick head count: There were at least four guards. Plus Kowalski, Ivan and Vladimir Grozny, and another shadow he could see moving in the office. Then there was Merrick. Would he side with Tommy if there was a fight? Could he fight at all anymore? Tommy gritted his teeth. He had been hiding for a hundred years. He was done hiding.

Tommy pulled his pistols from their holsters and cocked them. He knew the men standing over in the light couldn't see him, he had a steel pillar for cover, and their eyes were adjusted to the brightness of the glowing crucible. He had the element of surprise. He looked at the two people now on their knees, hands bound behind them, guns to their heads. It was his fault, his fault again. More innocents in danger. Another lost chance to find freedom.

"If you don't come out, they won't survive very long, Mr. McKinney. At least not in any way you'd recognize them. You have intentions of interfering, and as you know, I won't let anything stop our plan." Grozny was the one who sounded arrogant now. "You should be proud. We are going to use your friends to test the device tonight. They will be the first true converts to our faith. What the master always wanted." Grozny pulled a brass box from his coat pocket, not much larger than a smart phone. It wasn't a device that Tommy had seen before. "Do you recognize this? No? It is very ancient, many centuries old. It is a perfect mind control tool. I stole it from Adolf Hitler myself. He used it to bend an entire nation to his will." He stepped toward Katrina. "Your doctor friend will be first." He grabbed her by the throat and pulled her to her feet. She stood there frozen as he fiddled with knobs on the device.

In one quick motion he grabbed her throat and pressed the box against her forehead. Katrina screamed. Her whole body trembled like a seizure. Tommy couldn't let this happen.

"Stop! I'm coming out." Tommy stepped from the shadows with his gun dangling from the middle finger of his right hand.

He was surrounded by guards. There were three with AK-47s and one with an assault shotgun. He recognized two of them as the cops he had dealt with days before. All the men had their guns leveled at him. Tommy could see Merrick on the catwalk. He watched for a moment before returning to his work.

Katrina was screaming. "No! Don't do it! You can't trust him!"

Tommy kneeled down and set the pistol on the ground by the barrel and stepped back from it.

As the guards started to move in, Katrina turned and screamed at Grozny. "He carries two guns!"

There was no time to think. Tommy pulled his second pistol out and fired. The round hit Katrina in the back of the neck. She fell forward into Grozny. The Russian wasn't ready for it, and stumbled backward. Tommy turned and fired two shots at Ivan, but as he fired, he saw Scotty fall with the left half of his face blown off by a point-blank shot. Ivan fell, too. The first shot caught him in the leg. The second caught him in the chest as he fell. Tommy rolled to his right and ended up face to face with the fast cop. He fired with the barrel up against the man's chest. The bulletproof vest was no match for a high power round.

Tommy spun left and caught the second on the fly. The shot threw the cop off balance as he ran for cover and sent him careening into a steel pillar.

There was thunderous boom. Tommy felt indescribable pain in his right leg. The guard with the shotgun had gotten a round off. He rolled forward to where his other pistol lay. Grabbing it, he fired with both guns into the guard's chest.

The last guard let go with his AK. He missed Tommy, spraying the floor with lead as Tommy rolled back toward the first dead cop. Landing on his left side, he fired right handed from the floor, the first round clipping the guard's shoulder, the second impacting the center of his throat. Blood sprayed from the wound.

Kowalski had managed to get his gun out from under his gut. Tommy spun in place on the floor, fanning two rounds into the cop's chest before taking aim and landing the final shot between his eyes.

From nowhere the room was filled with sparks and heat. Merrick had dumped the crucible into the slag pit in the floor. The molten tin in the tray above it began to boil with the extra heat.

He saw motion from the corner of his eye: Grozny was limping for the stairs. Tommy struggled to his feet and aimed both pistols. Two clicks. Empty chambers.

Grozny heard it, too. He turned, a grin spread across his face. He lifted his pistol with his good hand and took aim. Tommy knew he couldn't dodge it. The Russian's expression changed as he pulled the trigger. The bullet cut through Tommy's shoulder, missing anything important. Tommy barely noticed. The scene before him had his full attention.

A mechanical hand had Grozny by the back of the neck. It lifted him from the ground and slammed him back into it. Coming down hard on his ruined knee, he howled in pain. Adalai Merrick stood over him with a terrible scowl on his face. He reached down and picked the horrified man up by the throat with that brass arm. Shots rang out. Grozny emptied his clip into Merrick, but the monster barely flinched. He kicked over a large barrel, dumping a liquid all over the floor. He picked up two nearby buckets from the floor with his human hand started slinging a fluid all over the room.

Grozny was panicking, struggling against the inhuman grip. Some of the liquid landed near

Tommy and he understood why Grozny was fighting so hard. It was kerosene.

Merrick's raspy whisper was now a vicious growl. "A hundred years you've kept me in Hell, now you'll burn with me." Merrick ran forward and fell into the slag pit, knocking the tray of molten tin into the growing pool of flammable liquid spreading across the floor. The concrete seemed to explode as the two met. As they disappeared into the flames Grozny's screams echoed through the empty building.

The fire spread through the old building like tinder. Tommy had no idea how much fuel was kept in this building, but there were flames everywhere, and they were growing.

On the catwalk that led toward the back of the building from the office, Tommy saw a dark figure running away from him. The last man in the office. They were separated by the fire. There was no way for Tommy to reach him. As the man reached the fire escape, he turned. In the glow of the flames, Tommy saw a face. That bearded, dark menacing face that had haunted his dreams for a century. Rasputin.

Tommy tried to run after him, but his leg gave out at the first step. No more than half a minute had passed since the shooting started, and he knew he had already lost a lot of blood. He saw the flames were reaching the roof now; it was only a matter of time before the whole building collapsed from the heat. Tommy turned and hobbled out the way he had come in.

By the time he made it to his car outside the fence, the police and fire departments were out in full force. The building would hopefully be a total loss, taking the bodies and the now useless brass with it. He laid a towel on the seat of his old Jag and drove back to the Basilica.

* * *

A month later, Tommy sat in the Rectory of Our Lady of Victory Cathedral. Father Daniel was speaking Latin into the phone. He hadn't spoken it in years, but Tommy got the gist of the conversation. The old priest put down the receiver.

"We've protected you as best we could. When the church learned about the return of the Khlysty, they were more than happy to cover for you when it came to the fire. I still think you should take their offer of a new life in Switzerland." His voice trailed off. "I'm just sorry neither of us could save Katrina"

"I did save her. From becoming one of them, from a life of mindless servitude to a broken faith. I don't need a new life, Father. I need to finish the old one first."

"Where will you be going?"

"We both know it's too dangerous for me to stay here. Eventually they'll figure out who I am, link that to all the lead I threw around, and the police will be after me for the murders. I have to clear out. Probably head south for a while." Tommy slipped on his overcoat. "Good luck to you, Father, and thank you again."

"You're welcome, my son. Keep in touch."

"I will, Father. Goodbye." Tommy adjusted his fedora and stepped out of the office.

As he walked to his Jag, Tommy felt that feeling again, on the back of his neck, like someone watching him. Of course, after the past few weeks, it was probably paranoia. He shrugged it off and started the engine. Pulling away from the curb, he saw a man in a tweed suit standing on the sidewalk in front of the church.

The man in the tweed suit noticed him, too.

Thomas McKinney, wanted for murder on three continents and in three centuries. The killer of a fellow Pinkerton agent in 1897. The man who had disfigured him. He finally found him.